Keeping Corner

Keeping Corner

KASHMIRA SHETH

DISNEP • HYPERION BOOKS

NEW YORK

Printed in the United States of America
First Disney • Hyperion paperback edition, 2009
3 5 7 9 10 8 6 4 2
This book is set in 13-point Deepdene.
Library of Congress Cataloging-in-Publication Data on file.
ISBN 978-0-7868-3860-8
Visit www.hyperionbooksforchildren.com
V475-2873-0 10218

In loving memory of my great-aunt Maniben Trivedi,
who lived her life with courage and dignity;
and for my parents, Bharatiben and Arvindbhai Trivedi,
who kept her story alive

GUJARAT, INDIA

1918

FINALLY, I COULD hear the bells on our bullocks' necks as Lakha hitched them to the cart. I peeked inside my mother's room. She was twisting her hair into a bun. "Hurry, Ba, hurry. I don't want to be late." I danced like a peacock, showing off my purple *ghagri-poulka*, a long skirt and a blouse.

"Don't fly away in your frenzy, Leela. The fair will be here for five days, and you'll have plenty of time to have fun."

"I want to buy my new bangles and ribbons before they're all picked over."

Ba raised her hand as if to slow me down. "*Khami ja*, I still have to change my clothes."

I opened her wooden cupboard and pulled out a sari. "Wear this one." It was my favorite because it had bands of vermilion, indigo, and turmeric stretching the length of it. The pattern was called *lahariu*, waves, and it was breeze-light and festival-bright. I liked bright colors on Ba because her silky black hair contrasted with them and made her sparkle.

I twirled the sari around myself until I was caught inside it. Ba unwrapped it. "*Saru*, fine." Then she picked up my ivory-colored *odhani*, scarf, and draped it over my shoulder. "Wait outside. I'll be right there."

I hurried through the back corridor. Only last week I'd helped Ba cover its floor with a fresh layer of dried cow dung and mud. I'd traced the half-moon shape and the peacocks' feet patterns Ba had showed me how to make with the heel of my palm and outstretched fingers. The two of us had finished overlaying the entire floor in one morning.

In the backyard, Lakha, who took care of our animals, was spreading a blanket on the floor of the cart. His long arms moved swiftly, and the tiny mirrors on his embroidered vest and cap twinkled. I could hear his voice but didn't understand what he was saying. Lakha hardly spoke more than a few words to people, but he talked to the bullocks and buffaloes all the time. I tiptoed behind him.

I always wanted to make him jump when I snuck up on him, but it never happened. Ever since I was little, I had tried creeping like a tigress following a spotted deer, but he was always ready for me. Could he feel the tremors of the earth and air before I uttered a word?

"Ready to take me?" I said close to his right ear.

He didn't jump or even turn around. "Are you wearing new anklets?" he asked in his deep, steady voice.

I didn't reply. He faced me, and I was annoyed to see laughter in his eyes. He held out his hand. I ignored it, lifted my ghagri slightly, and climbed onto the cart myself.

I pulled my knees close and wrapped my arms around them, looking down at my exposed feet and ankles. I admired my silver toe rings and fingered the anklets. *Choon-choon, channan, choon-choon,* they sang. I was so used to the tinkling of bangles and anklets that I didn't think about how loud they could be. No wonder Lakha had heard me coming.

I looked toward the back door. Where was Ba? A butterfly fluttered close to the cart, delicate and shimmery as a full-moon sky. I glanced at Lakha, who was staring into the horizon. "Lakha, what will you do at the fair?" I asked.

"I will talk to my friends."

"How do you know they will be there?"

"They will be there. Besides, I'm taking two of them with me."

I played with the clasp of my anklet, and it came

off. I dangled it in my hand. "I'm not your friend," I teased.

"I'm not talking about you."

I guess he meant the two bullocks.

He patted his friends, then opened the wide wooden back gates. As he pulled the cart out, I saw Ba. Lakha closed the gate after her.

"Can you put this on?" I asked Ba once she had climbed in the cart and sat down across from me.

"Don't play with the clasp. If it gets loose, you'll be sorry."

"I didn't do anything. It just came off."

Lakha was ready to drive the cart and had taken the bridle in his hand. He shook his head without glancing back at me. He had seen me playing with the clasp but would never tell on me.

Bapuji, my father, assumed we'd walk to the fair, but I hadn't wanted to. I had told Ba, "By the time we walk the two miles to the fair, my ghagri will be covered with dust, and I'll be too tired to have fun. Besides, we would have to leave so *early*. Can't you ask Bapuji if Lakha can take us?"

Ba had convinced Bapuji. It was always that way. I'd talk Ba into cooperating with what I wanted, and she'd talk Bapuji into approving.

At the end of the street where the four corners

met, Lakha stopped the cart suddenly. I got up on my knees to see what was happening.

"You'll be thirteen soon and must behave like a young woman. Don't gawk," Ba said.

"I was just looking—"

Before I could finish the sentence, we saw a white man and three Indian men riding on horses. Even though the white people ruled us, they rarely visited small towns like our Jamlee. Last year, when a white lady came to our school, all the men and women stood under the banyan tree just to get a glimpse of her. It was the first time a white woman had come to our town.

The *Engrej*, Englishman, passed close by me. I held my breath. I could have touched his leg if I'd wanted to. Ba and Lakha were quiet. So were the shoppers and the shopkeepers. Even our bullocks didn't move their heads, so their bells were silent. One of the Indian men was pointing at the big banyan tree in the middle of the *chokdi*, square, and talking in *Engreji*; I couldn't understand what he was saying.

"Why is he here?" I whispered.

"He is here to inspect how much damage we've had from the drought," Ba whispered back.

When they were farther down the street, we began moving again. I turned around to take a good look at the back of the Engrej.

Ba slapped my leg gently. "You're not a child any-more."

"I want to see if he keeps a stick of bamboo down his back. He looks so stiff."

"You must not flutter and fly like a wild bird. It won't be long before you have your *anu* and go to your husband's house."

Lately, Ba had been telling me not to laugh and sing loudly and not to jump when I was excited. All because I was going to live with my husband, Ramanlal, and his family. Ba's nudging and scolding annoyed me.

I had been engaged when I was two years old, and married at nine. And next year I am going to have my *anu*, a ceremony to send me to Ramanlal's house. We will invite him and his family, and I will get to wear a new sari and gold jewelry. A priest will chant Sanskrit mantras for the safe journey to my husband's house and through life. We will celebrate by singing and eating good food, then I'll leave the cocoon of my family and fly off to make a new home. Before I enter their house, Ramanlal's *ba* will welcome me with flowers and gifts. I am glad Ramanlal is from Jamlee. That way I don't have far to go.

Like my classmates, I knew I wouldn't go to school after my anu. Last year there were only five girls in my class. Then two of the girls had their anu and didn't come back to school. I wasn't invited to their ceremonies because they are from different castes. My family is *brahman*, the highest caste, and we can't eat food made by non-brahmans.

Last summer I went to my cousin Jaya's anu. Dressed in her shimmering sari and jewelry, Jaya looked like she had descended from the stars. Her arms were covered with colorful bangles, and women fed her sweets all day.

Jaya is older than I am and gets to do everything first. It's irritating. Her first baby tooth came out before mine did; she could fetch water from the well before I could; she learned how to read and write before I did. But I don't mind that she had her anu first. After all, I'm going to be with Ramanlal and his family for the rest of my life—so I want to stay with my family as long as I can.

I have heard people say, *Daughters are someone else's treasure, and the sooner you part with them the better off you are; daughters look good only in their in-laws' house,* and *the younger you marry your daughter the quicker you're done with your obligations.* I don't think those things are true. I can't imagine my family being relieved on the day they give me my anu.

Compared to our neighbors and relatives, our family is small. Bapuji's older brother, my *kaka*, and his wife, my *kaki*, have no children. My brother, Kanubhai, is twenty-one. He lives in Ahmedabad and just started

{ 9 }

teaching at a college. When Kanubhai was five, a holy man blessed him, saying, "You will grow up to be a learned man." So Bapuji refused to arrange Kanubhai's marriage until Kanubhai had finished his studies. Kanubhai graduated last year, and Ba was anxious for him to get married, but he said that he'd wait until after my anu.

The cart was moving along at a good pace, which I liked because the ride was fast and bumpy. I saw a clump of gooseberry shrubs that had lost all their leaves in the drought, exposing their tangled, thorny branches. Only the banyan, mango, *kesuda*, and other big trees were still green. But even their leaves looked dull, as if too much sun had bleached out their color. Except for the dusty streets, our town was usually lush. "Will all this turn green when the rain comes?" I asked Ba.

"I hope so."

This past monsoon season, the first rain came by the end of June, so Bapuji and Kaka plowed and planted our farm. Then we waited and waited. There was little rain for the entire three months of monsoon. Our harvest was barely enough to feed us. All we could do now was wait for the next rainy season, which came only once a year. I had heard that a long time ago, Jamlee had had seven years of drought. I couldn't imagine what would happen if our crops failed seven years in a row. "What if the rains don't come again?"

Ba's face turned gloomy. "Then famine would ravage everything. Even the big trees would suffer."

I didn't like to think about it.

A familiar voice shouted, "Wait, wait for us."

It was my *masi*, Ba's younger sister. She and her friend Heeraben were walking to the fair. Lakha stopped the cart, and the ladies scrambled up. Masi has a round face and small ears, like Ba. Her curly hair had escaped her bun and looked messy.

"Where are the boys?" Ba asked Masi.

"They went to the fair with their cousins hours ago," Masi replied.

I was relieved. Masi had three sons between the ages of six and ten. If they had been with her, our poor bullocks would've had even more weight to pull.

Words would pour out of Masi like the endless hum of crickets in the night. As soon as the bullocks started moving, Masi's tongue did, too. "Sister, look at that mango tree. The flowers are so small that you can't even see them. In a good year, they say a thousand blossoms yield a hundred mangoes; we'll be lucky to get even fifty this year."

Ba and I had already talked about the drought, and I didn't want her to worry more. So I turned to Ba, "Tell Masi about the new sari Kanubhai gave you."

Masi's eyes brightened as she tucked her hair behind her ear and looked expectantly at Ba. Masi's mother-in-law was stern and wouldn't allow her to buy frivolous things like clothes, or jewelry that wasn't made of gold. Masi borrowed Ba's saris all the time, and was thrilled when Ba got a new one. It meant she would get to parade a new sari in front of her mother-in-law without disobeying her.

We passed three young couples as we rode. The men walked slightly ahead of the women. One of the women carried a child on her hip, and another held a young girl's hand. Two identical boys scampered along.

"The one carrying the child is pregnant again," Heeraben said. "Those twins are hers, too. And her mother-in-law refuses to take care of a single one."

"She looks tired," I said, noticing that the woman was falling behind.

"That's what having four children in five years will do to you. Make sure you don't do that, Leela," Masi said.

Heeraben smiled in approval. Before I could reply, Ba said, "Leela, look on your side."

We were coming to the top of a hill. On the left was the Taransi River and Lord Shiva's Temple. "Ba, it's beautiful," I said, pointing to the fairground by the river. It was filled with shades of crimson and ocher, emerald and indigo from the women's saris and the men's turbans.

The shrill call of a langur monkey punctured the air, followed by more calls. The distant trees seemed to come alive with the group of langur traveling through the canopy. I squinted my eyes, looking for white fur, but couldn't see a single monkey. A flock of green parrots flew overhead, their red beaks streaking the sky.

Lakha dropped us at the fair in the front of the Lord Shiva Temple on the bank of the Taransi. Because of the drought, the wide waters of the river had shrunk to a trickle. I lifted my ghagri slightly with one hand, held Ba's hand with the other, and walked into the fair.

On the right side of the temple, a man made *jalebis*. First he fried batter made of white flour, then he dunked the hot circles in sugar syrup. Several people stood near him, waiting to be served. Masi and Heeraben stopped to talk to someone they knew. I was glad Ba kept walking.

There were women selling fruit: *bors*, papayas, black and white *shingodas*, and finger-long bananas. Farther down, the vendors offered idols, rosaries made of holy *rudraksh* beads, and utensils of brass and copper. I held onto Ba's hand and walked past all of them. Someone waved a burning stick of incense near my face. Ba took a deep breath and slowed down.

"Come, Ba, let's get the bangles first," I said, pulling her hand.

"This is the last package," the man with the burning incense said. "No one else here will have this fragrance—the essence of Kashmiri roses." Ba took another deep breath and stopped.

I glowered at the man and pulled Ba.

"I'll come back," Ba said to the man as we hurried away.

I was finally kneeling in front of the basket filled with *lakkh*, shellac bracelets of every color in a peacock's feather, in the sky at sunset, in shades of raw and ripe mangoes. The man looked at my wrists and, without measuring, picked out a set of bracelets and slipped them on my arm. They fit perfectly, but I didn't like their orangey-brown color. He showed me three or four more sets, but I didn't want any of them, either.

Then he took out a pair wrapped in newspaper. As he unwrapped the paper, I read the word WAR on it. Every day there was something in the paper about the war being fought across the oceans. I didn't really understand how we were a part of it when our land was not being attacked. Bapuji said it was because the British ruled us and they were at war, so we had no choice but to help pay for it. The war was a big fire that had to be fed first, and that meant we had a shortage of many things. Besides fuel, everyday purchases like sugar, wheat, and cloth cost more now.

The man slipped the bracelets onto my wrist. They were shiny red with yellow dots.

I turned to Ba. "I like these."

"But you just got here. Don't you want to try a few more?"

"These are what I want."

"Are you sure?"

"Yes."

After Ba paid the man, he asked me if I wanted the bracelets wrapped up.

I shook my head. "I want to wear them."

Then Ba went back to buy her incense, and after that we walked all around the fair. We stopped to listen to a *manbhatt*, a copper pot player. The pot gleamed in the sunlight. The manbhatt used a small ring to coax a variety of sounds from the pot. Some were sharp and thin like the end of a lance, others were dull and wide like a bullock cart. We listened until he was done playing a piece. When I put some change in his bowl, he said, "You can try."

He handed me a ring. I hit the pot at various places and made different sounds, but I couldn't make music.

Farther down on the side of the temple I picked out a pair of red and gold strings with tassels to braid in my hair. When we finished going around once, I was surprised to see two girls with shiny glass bangles.

"Where did you get those?" I asked.

They pointed toward a man sitting close to the wall of the temple. He was in the shadows so I hadn't noticed him when we went around the first time. I squeezed Ba's hand. "Let's see what he has."

"You already bought bracelets," Ba said. Her voice was irritated and she wore a frown on her face.

I sighed. "I know, but the glass ones are so delicate and pretty."

"I'm not going to buy you any more."

"How about if we just look at them?" I said, hoping Ba would change her mind once I slipped them on my arms.

I kept walking, with Ba only a step behind me.

When I squatted to get a closer look at the bangles, I saw the ones I wanted. They were the same shade of red as the ones Ba had just bought and were as thin and delicate as sun rays and splashed with dots of gold paint. I looked at my hand. These would fit perfectly between the two lakkh ones I was wearing.

"Ba, aren't these beautiful?" I asked.

The man's face was lined with thin creases. He picked up a few bangles with his knobby fingers and handed them to Ba. She lifted them up and moved out of the shade to see the sunlight passing through them. That way she could tell how good the glass was.

I took a bracelet off my right arm. He slipped the six glass bangles on my wrist. I slid my bracelet back on. "The perfect set," he said.

I extended my hand to show to Ba. I could tell from her eyes that she liked the way they filled my arm. As she counted the money, she mumbled, "I don't know why I spoil you so much."

The man said, "If you can't be soft with your daughter, who can you be soft with?"

Now that we had finished shopping, I was hungry. We stopped at the stall, and Ba asked the cook if he was brahman. The cook said yes, pointing to the *janoi*, sacred thread, that he wore over his right shoulder. We bought *papdi*, fried crisp wafers made of chickpeas that were served with raw papaya slices and green chilies sautéed in mustard oil. As the man served us papdi he said, "My brother has a jalebi stand by the entrance. Make sure to get some."

Ba smiled at him and nodded. While eating, we watched a *madari* and his pet monkey. The monkey was dark with white marks on his face and a long tail. At his master's command he did somersaults, danced, and did other tricks. At the end of his performance he gave a salute like the Indian men gave to their Engrej bosses, then came around with a cap to collect money. Ba gave me a coin, and when I dropped it in the monkey's cap, he gave me another salute. By the time the show was over, I had eaten all the green chilies, and the roof of my mouth was on fire. I glanced at the man frying jalebis. "If I could just eat one jalebi, my mouth would stop burning," I said to Ba.

She smiled as if she approved of my reasoning. She handed me a silver rupee. "Go get a half dozen and bring back the change."

Ba and I took the jalebis and sat in the temple's courtyard. I had eaten only one when I saw a young boy watching me. His dark and deep-set eyes looked sad. I still had two of my jalebis left, so I walked over and offered them to him. He refused at first, but I stood there with my arm outstretched until he took them. He smiled, and I could see he was missing his two front teeth.

Ba shared her jalebis with me.

After we finished eating, we went inside the temple. People were coming in for *aarti*, to pray together. The priest lit a brass *divi*, lamp, that held twenty-five flames of light. Then the musicians began playing cymbals, drums, and flutes, and people started to sing. The priest moved the divi in an alternating circle and semicircle. All around the temple, the music echoed, the shadows of golden light danced, and the Sanskrit verses twined.

Once aarti was over, the sun had already set and the fair had been lit with lanterns. It was time to go home. As Ba and I walked down the temple steps, I saw Fat Soma and his wife, Pushpa, holding hands. Fat Soma and Ramanlal had been best friends in school, and I had known Fat Soma forever because his grandfather and my grandfather were brothers. Despite his name, Fat Soma was not fat, but he had been until he was seven. Everyone except for his grandmother still called him Fat Soma. On the first day of school, when his teacher addressed him as Soma, he politely asked to be called *Fat* Soma.

Fat Soma and Pushpa let go of each other's hands the instant they saw us. When they stopped to talk to us, Ba said, "Fat Soma, I will not tell your parents."

Pushpa's cheeks turned red with embarrassment, and she pulled her sari over her forehead out of respect for Ba. Fat Soma glanced at her, then us, and smiled. His crooked tooth poked out a bit.

It was getting darker every second, and we didn't see Masi and Heeraben. "Let's go to the cart," Ba said. "If they are there, we can take them home."

They were waiting by the cart. I showed Masi my bangles.

Masi fingered them. "Pretty. They fill your arm nicely. What else did you get?"

"I got something to put in my hair, and we ate jalebis," I said.

"Of course you did, Princess Leela! When you go to your in-laws' house you will be sorry for all the pampering—"

"So what if I get her a few more things?" Ba said. "Between the two brothers, our family has only one daughter."

"That doesn't mean you should throw money on her every whim. Instead of buying all this useless stuff, you should have saved the money. Last year we bought more gold than you did, and we have many more mouths to feed than you. How did we do it? By living frugally and not spending on breakable little trinkets. When you sell gold, you get your money back; when you sell trinkets, you get nothing."

I glanced at Ba. She was quiet. I turned to Masi. "You can buy all the gold you want. I'd rather wear these pretty things than gold."

Masi stared at me for a second, then turned her face away. Ba sighed deeply. I stared out in the darkness. I knew Ba felt sorry that Masi's mother-in-law was so strict and controlling, but it bothered me that Masi scolded Ba every chance she got. It was as if Masi were the older sister. I wished Ba would tell Masi to keep her wisdom to herself.

Lakha let us out by the front gate before taking the bullock cart around back. Bapuji and Kaka were sitting with a few other men under the kesuda tree on *khatlis*, bed frames made of teakwood and laced with sturdy jute strings. Men often gathered in our courtyard in the evening, since it was so large and was right across from *Ramji Mandir*, the Lord Rama Temple.

Because of the war we couldn't use much fuel, so there were only a few lanterns casting a small light on the men's faces, and large shadows all around them. Bapuji looked in our direction, and the light bounced off his wide forehead. Kaka waved his hand at me. I waved back. One of the men said, "I don't understand what Gandhiji can do about our drought problem."

"He is asking the *sarkar*, government, to let go of our taxes, and we must be grateful to him," Bapuji said.

Gandhiji's real name was Mohandas Gandhi, but out of respect people called him Gandhiji. He had established an *ashram*, a communal living place, on the bank of the Sabarmati River near the city of Ahmedabad. I had heard Bapuji, Kaka, and other men mention his name often, because Gandhiji was always fighting for the rights of poor farmers and laborers.

"This British are as solid as the Himalayas. Why

would they listen to a little man like Gandhiji?" I heard someone say as I walked toward the house.

"He may be a small man but he is fearless. Last year Gandhiji was in Bihar speaking with farmers. When the sarkar threatened to arrest him if he didn't return home—saying he was an outsider in Bihar—he replied, 'You have come from five thousand miles away and consider yourself insiders, but I am an outsider because I have come from Gujarat? I will not obey your order.' And he didn't," Bapuji said.

"Remember, no one can build an empire by being compassionate. The sarkar will not let a single *pye* go."

The image of the Engrej on the horse came to my mind. He looked so unyielding. Would people like him show mercy and waive the taxes?

TWO

VASANT had arrived, marking the beginning of spring. Every year at this time we would put away heavy blankets, take out light cotton ones, give them a good shake, and spread them in the sun to get rid of the musty smell.

All day I ate puffed barley and candy that Kaki had bought for the festival. The candy was white, flat as saucers, and came strung in a garland. Our community was going to light a bonfire at dusk in the temple court-yard. Since our house was right across from the Ramji Mandir, we didn't have far to go to enjoy the fire.

One afternoon, after the festivities had died down, I watched while Kaki made a new silk cover for my blanket. It was made up of many shades of blue: from soft water to spring sky to dark rain cloud. When Ba came out of the kitchen, I pointed at the cover

Kaki was making for me. "Isn't this beautiful, Ba?"

A smile spread on Ba's face, but she was worried. "Won't all this pampering become a burden for Leela when she goes to her in-laws' house?" she asked Kaki.

Kaki put the fabric down. Her eyes were commanding and her voice was clear. "Ramanlal's mother will treat Leela like a daughter. She is quite attached to her. But even if she doesn't, let the girl enjoy herself. Childhood is short, so there's nothing wrong with making it sweet."

While Kaki sewed, Ba and I finished airing the summer blankets and spread them on the khatlis.

When all the work was done, I cut lemongrass, and Ba used it to flavor our tea, which the three of us drank before Kaki went to the temple.

I spread out my silk coverlet and was admiring it again when Masi walked in. She looked at it and then at me.

Her eyes grew wide. "For you?"

"Yes."

She turned to Ba. "Why do you indulge her so much?"

Ba avoided looking at Masi. "It's made from an old sari. Nothing fancy."

"You call it nothing? You could trade that sari for some brass pots instead of wasting it."

"Leela's kaki made it," Ba said.

Masi shook her head. "I never heard of a little girl who could make the whole family dance around her! Why don't you raise her the way girls are supposed to be raised? Our ba only indulged our brothers, never us sisters." Then she turned to me. "Leeladee, remember, if you climb up on the roof, you have to climb down, too."

I hated when Masi called me Leeladee. It rhymed with *beeladee*, cat. I was too happy to get upset, though. Besides, I wasn't going to walk into the trap she had set for me. She wanted me to say something sharp so she could prove I was spoiled. I smiled sweetly. "Masi, why don't you make one for yourself? Then we can both talk about how soft our covers are."

"I don't have expensive silk to waste," she said.

Ba offered her popped barley and some sugar candy. Masi didn't eat much of the popped barley, but she ate one piece of candy and took two pieces and tied them at the end of her sari. It seemed to pacify her.

"I heard that Fat Soma and Pushpa were behaving very badly at the fair," Masi said.

I picked up a piece of candy. "They were just holding hands." As soon as the words escaped my mouth I was sorry. What if Masi made a big thing out of it? I didn't want Fat Soma and Pushpa to get in trouble.

"You saw them?"

I pretended my mouth was stuffed with the candy and couldn't reply. Masi looked at Ba.

"They're young," Ba said.

Masi raised her eyebrows. "Yes. That's why they should show respect for their elders and not touch each other in broad daylight. Didn't you scold them?"

I started saying, "But—"

"Your ba and I are talking. Don't interrupt. Besides, what do you know about such things?" Masi said. "Go get me a glass of water."

I wanted to listen to them talk, so I walked to the kitchen slowly. I picked up a brass dipper hanging on a nail, dunked it in the earthen pot, then emptied the dipper into a tumbler, listening hard the whole time. When I brought the water out to Masi, she was whispering something to Ba. No wonder I couldn't hear what she was saying.

When Masi was done whispering, she took the tumbler from my hand and drank. She wiped her mouth with the back of her hand. "Will you do it?" she asked Ba.

"Fat Soma and Pushpa are respectful and caring people," Ba said. "I'm not going to tell on them."

"I wish I'd seen them holding hands instead of you, sister. I'd have complained to Fat Soma's ba."

Masi got up to leave as soon as Kaki returned. Masi

always turned sullen in Kaki's presence. Since Masi was my mother's sister and Kaki was my father's brother's wife, they were not related. Even I wasn't blood-related to Kaki. Masi felt that I should love and respect her more than Kaki since she was my mother's sister, but I couldn't. Kaki and I lived together, and she was like a second ba to me.

Kaki offered Masi candy and popped barley. Masi didn't refuse. She took two more pieces of candy and a fistful of barley. "We'll see you tonight at the bonfire," she said.

"Did you see the silk coverlet I made?" Kaki asked Masi.

"Yes, I did. It's very soft."

While the other women of Jamlee treated Kaki with respect, Masi complained to Ba about her. But Masi was never rude to Kaki's face. Did she fear her? Or was it that deep down Masi admired Kaki?

Masi wouldn't scold me in Kaki's presence, so I said, "Masi liked the coverlet so much that she might make one for herself." I turned to Masi and added, "If you do, don't forget to show it to us."

Masi glared at me but her mouth was shut tight.

I wondered what made Kaki so special. Maybe it was the way she carried herself. Even when she had three pots of water stacked one on top of the other on her head, she walked tall and straight, her hands swinging by her sides, matching the stride of her feet. Or maybe it was the way she spoke, softly but firmly, that demanded to be heard. Kaki was not a tall woman, but her heart and mind were strong, and it came through in her steady gaze.

Kaki never hesitated to punish me or Kanubhai if we misbehaved. If she hit your cheek with the back side of her palm, it would sting for hours. Luckily, she'd only scolded me, but she had hit Kanubhai once when he was eight and had played a trick on his teacher.

The afternoon melted into evening as I watched the blossoms of the kesuda tree float softly to the ground. Ba said it was time to get ready. She oiled and combed my hair with a fine-toothed sandalwood comb, then braided it. I washed my face and neck. Just as I was done wiping my face, a group of boys, including Fat Soma, came to the house asking for firewood. They had jute bags to carry the wood in. Kaki told them to take some wood from the shed behind Lakha's hut.

The boys' laughter filled the house for a few seconds. I never used to look at the boys who came to gather firewood, but today I watched them out of the corner of my eye as Kaki gave them each a fistful of popped barley and a piece of candy. I wanted them to linger a little longer. And I wished Ramanlal was here in town instead of away at college in Ahmedabad.

Soon Kaka and Bapuji returned from the field and went to take their baths. I smoothed out their white *dhotis* so they wouldn't be wrinkled when they wrapped them around their waists. The dhotis Bapuji and Kaka wore to the farm were rough and thick, but the ones they wore to go out in were soft and fine.

Lakha milked the cows and buffaloes early, and then it was time for all of us to go to Ramji Mandir.

Orange-red tongues of flame leaped up from the large bonfire. I looked around. The faint light of dusk was smothered by the black smoke rising from the many fires around Jamlee. The faces of people standing close to the fire were colored with its glow. In one corner I saw two widows, their brown saris melting into the darkened shadows.

There were many coconuts in the fire, and Fat Soma and the other boys removed the cooked ones with iron rods. Once they cooled down, the boys cracked them open and gave us pieces to eat. We also had roasted yams and potatoes. The yams were sweet and smoky, and I ate two of them.

Fat Soma's youngest sister, Puri, waved me over. Puri had a small nose, but she could sniff out gossip from miles away. When I got close to her, she stood on her tiptoes and whispered, "Did you know Ramanlal is coming home soon?"

Puri was two years younger than I was, and it was annoying that she knew things about Ramanlal before I did. So I told her I already knew.

"Who told you? Ramanlal?" Puri's mouth opened up, round as a well.

"Who told *you*?" I asked.

"My brother."

I wanted to ask Puri why Ramanlal was coming and how long he was staying, but I couldn't now. Puri had three older sisters and one brother, so she always knew what was going on in Jamlee. Sometimes I wanted to pinch her hard for being all-knowing and all-wise. It wasn't a nice thought and I never did it, but I wished I could.

She put her hands on her waist and pouted. "Who told you?"

The fire had shrunk, and people were leaving. Ba called, "Leela, *chalo*, let's go."

I ran to Ba without answering Puri.

After dinner Kaka asked me to bring his *tanpura*, a one-string instrument. I got it from his room and gently carried it out. We sat on the floor of the *chauk*, patio, and Kaka played music. We all took turns singing. This night was special because the air was filled with smoky haze from the fires, and the full moon kept peeking in and out of the clouds. Our voices rose and rode on the breeze and whispered to the kesuda tree, whose leaves fluttered in reply.

All at once a cold wind picked up. "Where did this breeze come from?" Kaka said.

I snuggled up to Ba and tried to wrap part of her sari around me. "Leela, you're shivering!"

Bapuji got up and brought me my blanket. Before I knew it, I had fallen asleep listening to Kaka's music and Lakha's singing.

THREE

TWO DAYS LATER, Ramanlal's ba invited me to spend the day with them. I loved going to their house because I was allowed to wear a new ghagri-poulka even though it wasn't Diwali or any other holiday. And his ba would make my favorite food. Everyone told me I was blessed to have her, because a mother-in-law could make or break a girl's heart and life.

I wore my sunset-red ghagri-poulka and my new bangles. Ba braided my hair and tied the end with one of the strings we bought at the fair. Then I picked up the round silver box that sat on the shelf next to Ba's wooden cupboard. I opened the box and dipped my finger in the vermilion powder. Standing in front of the mirror, I made a *chandlo* in the middle of my forehead. It was a perfect circle.

Ba walked me to Ramanlal's house in the morning. On the way I wondered if Puri was right about Ramanlal coming home. I could feel my heart beating faster thinking about it. When we reached his house, Ba said, "Behave properly."

"Don't I always?"

"If you did, I wouldn't have to remind you. Two days ago you teased Masi about the silk coverlet. That is showing disrespect, not behaving. You're a young woman now. Know your limits and respect your elders. Don't laugh or talk loudly, offer to help in the kitchen, and be pleasant. Don't forget—this is your in-laws' house."

I nodded.

Ramanlal's ba came to the door and talked to Ba for a few minutes. I waited patiently by their side even though I wanted to go in the house and see if Ramanlal was there.

My mother-in-law's face was smooth, and her neck was slim and long. It made her look young. Standing close to her I realized that she was not much taller than I was. And I had a few more years to grow.

"Leela, remember what I told you," Ba said before leaving.

"Yes, Ba," I replied.

Puri was right. Ramanlal *was* home. He was dressed

in white and his hair was parted on the left side. He was not short like his ba, but he had her delicate features. His face was well scrubbed and his eyebrows arched perfectly. Had he groomed himself because I was coming, or had he always looked this way and I hadn't noticed before?

Even though I had gone to Ramanlal's house often, I had never talked to him or wanted to spend time with him, but today I realized that it wouldn't be long before I'd have my anu and come to live here. It made me nervous. All morning my heart was jumping, my hands were shaking, and my eyes hunted for glimpses of him.

Ramanlal and I couldn't talk to each other, and we couldn't be alone, but when our eyes met, my face burned with nervousness and excitement, and I smiled self-conciously. I noticed that Ramanlal's ba and grandmother were watching us. Maybe they had seen a change in me and were making sure we didn't do anything inappropriate. Or maybe it was me who kept my eyes on them, hoping to steal a moment or two with Ramanlal.

For lunch, Ramanlal's ba made my favorite: *pooranpoli*, bread filled with sweetened lentils and cardamom. I made the balls of sweetened lentil and handed them to her one by one. Ramanlal said he wasn't hungry and didn't eat until after his bapuji, grandfather, and grandmother had finished. When his ba, he, and I sat down to eat, he took a piece of pooran-poli and slipped it in my mouth when his ba wasn't looking. I was so shocked I couldn't chew. Except for Ba, Kaki, and Kanubhai, no one had ever fed me. It felt strange when Ramanlal did.

"Leela, don't you like my pooranpoli?" Ramanlal's ba asked.

I covered my mouth and swallowed quickly. "It's very good." I was afraid that she'd ask why my voice was quivering.

"Your words can lie but not your mouth. Eat it and I'll believe you like it."

"You're right," Ramanlal said. "How do we know she likes the food at our house if she doesn't eat it?"

She gave him a stern look. "You don't need to get in between women's talk." Then she smiled at me and whispered, "Don't tell men everything. Always keep them guessing how deep your river runs."

That afternoon, when everyone was taking a nap and I was sitting in the back corridor embroidering a tablecloth, Ramanlal came out of nowhere. "Is this for us?"

My heart raced and my voice faltered. I wanted to ask him why he had fed me pooranpoli at lunch, when he would be done with his studies, and if he was going to be bossy. All those thoughts got jumbled up in my head, and nothing came out of my mouth. Not even the answer to his question. All I said was, "What?"

He picked up the cloth. "Did your ba teach you how to embroider? This is beautiful. Bring it when you come after your anu."

"I don't know what I can bring with me."

"Don't worry about it. When you come, you will be bringing all I want."

I felt the blood rush to my face. I looked down. When I glanced at him from under my lashes, he was still watching me. He wanted me to come to his house. I couldn't stop smiling.

Why did I have to look at him? Why did I have to smile?

Ramanlal sat next to me and fingered my bracelets. I began to tremble, not with fear, but with excitement. Still, I moved my hand away. "What if your ba sees us?"

"She won't." Then he whispered, "I leave soon and I don't know when I'll be back. You won't forget me, will you?"

My heart swelled with feelings that I didn't know I had for him. "I . . . how could I? I'm married to you."

There was a tinkling of bangles. Was his ba coming?

He stood up and vanished as suddenly as he had appeared.

For the afternoon snack we had dried *kothimda*, a fruit of the vine that grew in monsoon. I was surprised that Ramanlal's ba served them, because the drought had made the fruit scarce. They were crisp and sprinkled with hot pepper and salt.

Ramanlal's ba combed my hair with a special fine-toothed comb that dispensed jasmine-infused oil. It was tingly and soothing at the same time. Then she braided my hair and put two silver barrettes in it.

"These barrettes belonged to me, and I want you to have them," she said.

"To take home?" I asked.

"Yes, take them home now and bring them back with you later. That way you can pass them on to your daughter or daughter-in-law." Then she asked, "What color sari do you want for your anu?"

"Whatever you choose," I said, keeping my gaze on the floor.

She lifted my face up with her fingers. "You'll have to wear it, so it would be better if you like it. Talk to your ba. I'll ask Ramanlal to stop at your house before he leaves, so you can tell him."

"I will." I turned my face away, for I was sure I was blushing.

After that, Ramanlal's grandmother and I fluffed some cotton that had been matted down. Side by side we worked, pulling the cotton apart until it was light and soft. Then we stuffed it into a new pillow.

When we were done, I watched her comb her silvery hair. "Will you come and help me make pickles when the green mangoes are ready?" she asked.

"I will. Bapuji says we have to wait at least two more weeks."

"Yes, and it's going to be small crop. I'll only make hot pickles this year, unless you like sweet ones." She pulled her hair into a bun. "Anyway, I thought it would be a good excuse to get you back here. Isn't it?"

"It is," I said, thinking how lucky I was to be married into such a loving family.

That night when Ba and I walked home, she asked what I had done all day.

I told her about the pooranpoli and kothimda, and how much I liked the silver barrettes Ramanlal's ba gave me. I told her that I could pick out the color of my sari, and that I would help make pickles, but I didn't say a word about Ramanlal. That night I tried to picture his face, but couldn't. He moved through my thoughts like a dream. He was there and not there, real and unreal, known and unknown.

*   *   *

The next day Kaki left to visit her brother for a month. After Bapuji and Kaka went to the farm, it was just Ba and me in the house. The next few months, until the start of monsoon, was the season for weddings and janoi. The janoi gave brahman boys the right to perform religious ceremonies and chant *Gayatri Mantra*, one of the most sacred mantras. It was traditional to invite the entire caste for these occasions, and almost every day there was something going on in our brahman community.

That evening we were invited for the janoi of some distant relative at the *dharmashala*, a community hall. Kaka hardly ever came to these functions, and Ba wasn't feeling well, so I went with Bapuji.

I wore a plumeria-colored ghagri-poulka with a lime-green georgette odhani that was embroidered with tiny mirrors. Ba gave me gold earrings, bangles, and a three-stranded necklace to wear. She braided my hair, twisted it into a bun, and slid in the silver barrettes that Ramanlal's ba had given me. After I got ready, Ba opened a silver box and dipped her finger in the kohl. She put a black mark in my hair near my right temple, saying, "You look beautiful. I don't want an evil eye on you."

I looked in the mirror and pulled out a few strands

of hair near my ears. I twirled them on my fingers until they hung like the tendrils of a kothimda vine. Bapuji caught me and said, "*Khali chano vage ghano,*" the emptier you are, the more sound you make. Quickly, I moved away from the mirror.

When Bapuji and I were near the dharmashala I could smell the whitewash that had been applied to the walls only a few days before. The arch of the entrance was adorned with a statue of Lord Ganesh. A long porch wrapped all around the building like a shawl wraps around shoulders.

Bapuji stopped by the entrance to talk to the elderly men of the host family. Puri came running to me and pulled my arm. "Come, Leela, come, I want to show you something."

"Go with her," Bapuji said.

"What is it?" I asked Puri as we entered the large rectangular space in the middle of the building, where women and children were already sitting on the earthen floor to eat.

"Your Ramanlal is here," Puri whispered. Her eyes sparkled as bright as her gold odhani.

"So?" I said, even though I was surprised that he was still in Jamlee.

The breeze carried the smell of cloves, ginger, turmeric, and cumin powder simmering in the soup. I'd never seen a man cook for his own family, but for weddings, death, and janoi ceremonies, only men cooked, and it was the job of young men from the community to serve.

All day long I had dreamed of food: peanuts simmering in a soup of spices and lentils, giving it crunch, potatoes in thick sauce served with fluffy, long rice. And of course, sweet *kansar*, a steaming, whole-wheat and brown-sugar dessert drenched in *ghee* and showered with powdered sugar on top. But now the food was not important; all I wanted was a glimpse of Ramanlal.

"Puri and Leela, don't stand in the middle of the floor like a couple of cacti. Find a place to eat and sit down," Masi said when she spotted us.

Puri whispered to me, "If you're a cactus, your masi is an even bigger one. With pointy thorns."

I laughed.

Then Puri folded her arms and raised her chin slightly. It made her look smug. "If you don't want to see Ramanlal, I won't tell you which side he is serving."

"Go sit in that row," Masi said, pointing us toward her right. "The sooner we eat, the sooner our men can eat."

"Tell me. I do want to see him," I whispered.

"Touch your ears."

I glanced around. I didn't want anyone to see Puri making me act like her pet monkey. No one was paying attention to us. I quickly touched my ears. Puri was satisfied.

"Follow me," she said, and walked clear across to the other side from where Masi had told us to sit.

We found a place at the end of the last row. I gathered my ghagri-poulka and sat carefully on the cotton rug so my clothes wouldn't touch the floor and get dusty. I tucked the edges of my ghagri under my crossed legs and waited to be served. A boy came around, passing us a *patral* and *padio*, a plate and a bowl made out of the leaves of the *khakhra* tree sewn together by thin twigs.

It seemed like every single person was talking at the same time. The place was full of sounds and echoes. I concentrated on the men carrying food out of the kitchen. Sweet was always served first, and there was Ramanlal with a brass platter heaping with kansar. I looked away. When Ramanlal served Puri, she stared at him, and I stole a quick look. He was so close, I could smell his perfumed hair oil and see the dark hair of his mustache. I could almost feel the folds of his silk dhoti, and before I could think more, he served me. He covered my whole patral with kansar. "Your hands dish out more than my stomach can fit," I whispered.

His eyes twinkled.

I glanced at Puri, afraid she was listening. The girl sitting on the other side of her asked Puri something, and she turned her face toward her. "You shouldn't have served me so much," I said to Ramanlal.

He bent down a little more and whispered in my ear, "I want to give you something."

Before I could answer him, someone said, "This row hasn't been served kansar yet. Who has it?"

Ramanlal went off to serve them.

"What did he say?" Puri asked.

"Nothing," I said, trying to keep my voice calm and disinterested.

"If you don't tell me what he said, I will tell your masi about it."

I didn't want Masi to know what Ramanlal had said to me, so I lied to Puri. "He said, 'Eat and grow up like a kothimda vine.'" And we both giggled.

"Boys don't know how to talk. All they know is how to whistle, fly kites, read, and count," she said, mixing the ghee, sugar, and kansar with her fingertips. "You will have your anu soon and then you'll have to do what Ramanlal tells you."

"No I won't," I said, thinking he wouldn't be mean to me. Not Ramanlal.

"My sisters know everything. They say after anu you have to obey your in-laws and please your husband."

"Does Pushpa do what Fat Soma tells her to do?" I asked.

"I don't know. They only talk at night when they're alone."

"How do you know they talk?"

Puri shrugged her shoulders.

"You don't know a lot of things because you're only ten and not married."

"I'm engaged. Besides, my sisters tell me everything."

I shook my head.

"They do," Puri said. "You're jealous because you don't have a sister, and even though your brother is older than mine, he's still not married."

"He will be, soon."

"Really?" Puri's eyes brightened.

I had no intention of backing down. "Sure."

We stopped talking as Ramanlal returned with a water jug and filled up my glass. He stood there for a minute, but I didn't dare look at him.

I could only eat half of the kansar Ramanlal had served me. Outside the back door of the dharmashala, untouchables were already lined up to take the leftover food. It would not go to waste.

After the other courses were done, Bapuji was helping to clean up, and I was tired, so Masi said she'd walk me home. I waited for her by the side door of the dharmashala. It was the fifth night after the full moon, and the sky held a bite of moon and countless stars. Occasionally, fireflies flickered on and off.

Suddenly, I detected a movement behind a *pipul* tree. Even though it was a warm night, I shivered, thinking about the stories I had heard about pipuls being the home of ghosts. My feet turned heavy as an elephant's, and I couldn't move an inch. Then Ramanlal emerged from behind the tree, holding a folded piece of paper. "Leela, read it and write back." It was hard to see the expression on his face, but his voice was as soothing and sweet as honey.

I wanted to take his letter, but I was afraid. What would my family say?

"Take it, please, before someone sees us," he pleaded.

"I can't. What if my family finds out?"

"It won't be long before they bring you to my house to live with me."

"Maybe you can give the letter to me then."

"Don't make me wait." He extended his hand. "Quick."

Before I could reach for the note, I heard Masi's voice. "Leela, are you out there?"

Then we both saw Masi coming out of the building, her face shining in the light of the lantern she was holding. Ramanlal slunk away before Masi saw him.

On the way home Masi talked about how much food was prepared that night and who cooked what and who ate the most kansar. I tried to ignore her.

A strong wind blew when I opened the front gate of our courtyard, shaking the limbs of the kesuda tree. My heart was just as shaky as those limbs.

When I went inside, Kaka was sitting in the chauk of our house playing tanpura. "*Bess*, sit," Kaka said. "Tell me, who did you see and what did you eat at the dharmashala?"

The stone floor of the chauk had cooled off, and I laid down a jute mat to sit on. I told Kaka about Puri and Masi and all the other people I had seen. I didn't mention Ramanlal. I told him about all the food I ate, and when I said kansar my heart quickened.

I talked to Kaka, but my mind was on the letter Ramanlal had offered. How I wished I had taken it.

The next morning I went to the well with Ba, then read the newspaper to Kaka. He had been having problems with his vision lately. I read him an article about Gandhiji interviewing the collector of Kheda and also helping mill workers in Ahmedabad. But when I finished I couldn't remember a word of it. All day long I did many things, but my heart remained fixed on the letter. What did it say? Why didn't I take it? Would Ramanlal try to give it to me again?

If he did, I was going to take it.

FOUR

THAT EVENING Ba and I were rolling dough made of cooked rice flour with cumin seeds and salt. The dough was sticky and I had to keep applying oil to my rolling pin. We let the rolled *kichus* dry, and that way they would keep for many months. When we wanted to eat a few, all we had to do was roast or deep-fry them. This year Ba let me make the dough because she wanted to teach me all the things I needed to know before I had my anu and went to live with Ramanlal.

I had just spread out a stack of kichus on a newspaper to dry when Fat Soma came running through the courtyard, arms flailing, spit foaming at his mouth, eyes bulging like he'd seen the *Yamraj*, the god of death.

"What is it?" Ba asked as she sprang up.

Fat Soma stood there doubled over, clutching his stomach.

"Leela, give him some water." Ba put her arm around him. "What's wrong? You breathe like your lungs are on fire."

I handed Fat Soma a brass tumbler of water. He gulped it down so fast it all came back out in spurts of coughing. The rolled-out kichus were ruined. *Can't you drink water properly?* I wanted to shout, but the way he looked at me and shook his head made my mouth dry up.

"Ramanlal," he said. "A snake bit Ramanlal."

A scream pushed up my throat. I kept it in by covering my mouth with both my hands.

"Our Ramanlal?" Ba gasped.

"Yes. It was a *kalotar*."

"No, no, no. This can't be true," I said, shaking my head. Kalotars were one of the deadliest snakes, and what if . . . The floor underneath my feet seemed to have moved. I sat. I wanted to ask Fat Soma where Ramanlal was, but fear had sucked out all my words. I couldn't make a sound.

Ba grabbed the wall. Her voice wobbled with fear. "Have they called Shamji?" Shamji was a *bhoova*, a medicine man, who knew special chants to bring the poison out of a victim's body.

"He is in Thasara. One of Ramanlal's brothers went for him, but by the time he gets there and brings the bhoova back, it might be . . ."

Fat Soma didn't need to finish. Time was a critical factor. If the venom spread, even the most learned bhoova couldn't do a thing.

My whole world turned as dark as the belly of a kalotar. Ba held me close. Both of us were trembling.

Everything was hazy and far away. "Who will tell Bapuji and Kaka?" I asked, without realizing what I was saying.

"I will go to your farm. Leela, keep courage." Fat Soma's voice was thick and uneven. I listened to the pounding of his feet until there was no more sound.

Ba lit a prayer lamp and kept adding ghee so the flame wouldn't go out. She wrapped her arm around me and recited *Rama Raksha Stotra*, a prayer to keep Ramanlal safe.

I closed my eyes for a few seconds and then opened them to see if I had been dreaming about Fat Soma telling me that Ramanlal had been bitten by a snake. But the half-finished kichus were still there.

Bapuji and Kaka went straight to Ramanlal's house. Later Bapuji came back to take Ba and me there. His face was grim, and in one day he looked as if he had aged many years.

"Did the bhoova come?" I asked.

"Not yet."

Before we reached Ramanlal's house, a piercing cry shattered the quiet of night. Ba held my hand tightly. Ramanlal had died before we got there. I barely had a glimpse of him before they ushered me to the back room. I sat in the corner with Ba, tears streaming down our cheeks. We were surrounded by other women. In the dim light I couldn't see their faces well, but I could hear their cries.

I don't know how long we sat there.

Dawn arrived, and I heard a faint chanting, "*Hare Rama, Hare Rama, Rama Rama Hare Hare,*" as if it rose from a deep well. I knew they were preparing Ramanlal's body for cremation. A woman came and held her hand out to me. Her hair was messy and her eyes were puffed up. I didn't recognize her.

She touched my hand and said, "*Chal.*" From the voice I knew it was Ramanlal's ba. She took me to Ramanlal. His body was covered with white sheets and lay on a bed frame made out of bamboo sticks and two long pieces of wood. His face looked peaceful, as if he were just sleeping. Someone handed me a plump, bright marigold garland to put around his neck. Ba guided my trembling hands.

Then a priest held up his hand, and Fat Soma, Ramanlal's father, his uncle, and Bapuji lifted the bed to carry the body to the cremation ground by the Taransi River. All the men would follow them, but the women would stay home.

Ramanlal's ba collapsed as they walked away. I fanned her with a bamboo fan. Slowly, the sound of the chant moved farther and farther away. Ba and the other women recited the name of Lord Rama.

I began chanting *"Hare Rama, Hare Rama"*—but my mind had wandered away. It had joined the funeral procession.

As Ba and I walked home, I thought about a funeral pyre I had seen once from a distance. The golden flames leaped skyward and then turned into black smoke, whirling away above the water of the Taransi while the chanting of the priests set the soul of the dead free.

Soon, the priest would perform the ceremony and cremate Ramanlal's body. I would never see him again. How I wished I had his letter.

But maybe it didn't matter, because now nothing mattered.

Bapuji and Kaka bathed when they came home after the cremation. They had not put on their shirts, and I could see that they were not wearing their janois over their right shoulders. From the wooden cupboard, Ba took out two new janois for them.

"I thought men only changed their janoi in monsoon," I said to her.

"And also after cremating a family member."

"I didn't know that."

Ba looked away. "There are many things you don't know," she mumbled.

Ba and I had never talked about it, but there was a saying that a widow's life was a living death. For the first year after a husband's death, a widow couldn't go out. So, except for attending Ramanlal's ninth-day ceremony, I'd have to stay in the house. It was called keeping corner.

That afternoon, Bapuji was as pale as a candlewick, Kaka turned into a silent stone, and Ba cried like her eyes were the skies of the monsoon. After drying her tears with the edge of her sari, Ba muttered, "O, Rama, this is not a small tear in my sari that I can repair. My soul has been ripped apart. What am I to do? O, Rama, what will I do with her?" and then she cried and shook until she was in a trance. I was afraid of her and wished Kaki had not gone away to her brother's house.

Ba slipped the gold bangles from my wrists. They were plain so I didn't mind taking them off, but I loved wearing my milk-glass bangles and the lakkh bracelets.

"A widow can't wear bangles," she said.

I knew that the bangles were a sign of a woman's

good fortune, and when your husband dies your fortune is gone, and you can never marry again. I looked at my hand. "When will you take the glass and lakkh ones off?" I asked.

Ba bit the end of her sari. "Another *widhwa* will have to take them off for you."

Another widhwa, I thought. Who's a widhwa? Then I realized that I was the widow. The word thumped in my head.

Ba put the gold bangles in the trunk where we kept all our gold jewelry. Later, one of our neighbors, Jivima, came. She was Kaki's friend and as old as the River Ganga. Her eyes were weak and she carried a cane. She always wore a brownish widow's sari called a *chidri*.

Ba took Jivima and me to the back of the house. Jivima picked up a stone. "Leela, put your hands down," she said in a trembly voice.

Ba held my hands, and Jivima hit the bangles gently.

"No," I moaned, but I couldn't move my hands away.

The broken bangles lay on the ground. I looked at my naked hands. Tears ran down my cheeks.

Then Ba took out one of her saris and told me to wear it instead of the blue one I had on. "You have to wear black until the ninth-day ceremony."

FIVE

BAPUJI must have sent a message to Kaki about Ramanlal's death, because she came home the next day. When I saw her open the gate, I felt hope. As she came closer, my hope slipped away like the heat I breathed on my hands to keep them warm on cold mornings.

Not only was Kaki wrapped in a black sari from head to ankle, but her face was different, too, as if it had lost something. It took me a few moments to realize what she was missing. It was her nose ring. Her face had dulled without it. Unlike Kaki, Ba wore a nose ring only on special occasions. Now that I was widowed, neither of them would ever wear one again. When there was a widowed daughter in the house, the elder women gave up wearing flowers, nose rings, and bright saris.

When Ba saw Kaki she started sobbing and sank to

the floor. Kaki held Ba's head in her lap and me in her arms. Unlike those of my other relatives, Kaki's tears fell silently on her cheeks and tumbled down her face, finally dropping onto her sari, where they were absorbed instantly. I'd never seen Kaki cry.

Bapuji sent messages to Kanubhai, and I knew he would come for Ramanlal's ninth-day ceremony.

"I took the bangles off right away," Ba told Kaki, "but we'll have to take the rest off before the ceremony. Will you help me?"

Without answering, Kaki unclasped my gold neck-lace, unscrewed my earrings, and tried to pull off my silver toe rings. Ba clenched the end of her sari in her fist and shoved the wad in her mouth. I could still hear her muffled cry.

The toe rings were tight and wouldn't come off. Kaki got a bucket of hot soapy water and had me soak my feet. She knelt in front of me and slipped off each one. Then she put a necklace made of *tulsi* beads around my neck. Since tulsi is considered one of the most sacred plants, the beads made out of it are holy. The gold necklace I used to wear had shone; the wooden necklace looked dull even in the bright sunlight.

I watched Kaki gather up my jewelry. I fingered the brown beads and mumbled, "From now on, only this is mine."

Kaki opened her palms. "They're still yours, even if you can't wear them."

I extended my hands, and Kaki put my jewelry in them. I gave the pieces one last look before I handed them back to her.

She tied them up in a handkerchief. "I'll save them. They're yours until you want to give them to someone."

If I can't wear them, what difference does it make who they belonged to? I thought. "I never want to see them again," I said.

She held me tight as if she were afraid of losing me.

Those first eight days were bundled up in Ba's tears, Bapuji's doleful eyes, and Kaka's downcast head. Only Kaki kept her courage.

Every afternoon Kaki would make tea for us. After we finished tea, she'd say to Ba, "We must get ready for the visitors."

They'd splash cold water on their faces and straighten their hair. Kaki would fill her small box with sniffing tobacco.

Every afternoon people would come for *kharkharo*, mourning. The women would cry with Ba and Kaki, and the men would smoke with Bapuji and Kaka in the front courtyard.

I didn't know what the men talked about because I

couldn't hear them, and I didn't understand much of what the women said because they kept crying and talking at the same time. I stopped paying attention after a while.

At night, when I rested my head in Kaki's lap, my mind wandered back to the life I had before Ramanlal died. The fairs, the festivals and celebrations, the visits to Ramanlal's house, and the letter I almost took, which could only live in my memory now. I had to accept that I was a widow. With my good fortune gone, I was scared of the things I would have to do, and sad for things I wouldn't be able to do.

Ba had a headache on the evening of the eighth day after Ramanlal's death. Kaki roasted cloves, ground them, and made a paste with water. Ba got headaches often, and when she did, she rubbed the clove paste on her forehead, tied it with a piece of cloth, and slept in a dark room until she felt better. Her room perpetually smelled of cloves.

I sat by Kaki after Ba went to sleep. She kept her eyes to the ground as if she were afraid to look at me, and took deep breaths as if she couldn't get enough air.

"Kaki, are you sick?" I asked.

"No," she said. "I don't know how to tell you this.

Tomorrow . . ." Before she could finish, she got choked up and tears rolled down her face. She put her hand over mine. "Your hair. We have to cut—"

"NO!" I said, and pushed her away.

"We must."

I looked at my hair, my beautiful hair: dark, thick, and curly like monsoon clouds. It came down almost to my waist. It was terrible that I had to give up all the jewelry. But at least I was not born with it. My hair was mine. God had given it to me. How could anyone take it away?

I was filled with so much rage, I wanted to shout and scream. If I didn't, I would go mad. "I won't let anyone touch my hair!"

"Leela, we have no choice but to follow the custom."

Our traditions were woven into our lives, and I enjoyed many of them, like celebrating Diwali, and other festivals. Festivals made everyone happy, but cutting my hair would make *me* miserable and bring joy to no one else. "Who started this? And why? Can anyone benefit from it?"

Kaki shook her head.

I realized that this was just a made-up rule, and something inside of me snapped. "I don't want to follow this custom. I want my bangles, my earrings, my ghagri-poulka. I want everything back. Everything."

My voice came out loud and trembled like I had no control over it.

Bapuji heard me and said, "A widow must learn to live like a widow."

"O, Rama," Kaka called out in despair.

I wanted to ask Bapuji why I had to suffer so much when I had done nothing wrong, but all I said was, "Yes, Bapuji." He was my father and I respected him.

I kept my eyes on the pale bands of skin on my toes where I used to wear silver rings. The day Kaki took off my toe rings the bands had been white and sharp, but they were slowly turning darker. In a few days they would disappear completely, and I wouldn't be able to tell where I had worn them. And as the bands faded, the phrase "A widow must learn to live like a widow" would become clear to me.

On the ninth day, before the sunrise, Nathu, the barber, came with his brass satchel. His face was grim and he avoided looking at me.

"Ba, do I have to?" I asked one last time.

"There is no other way."

"Can't you talk to Bapuji? I don't mind giving up all the jewelry, but let me keep my hair."

She was silent.

As Bapuji and Kaki walked me to the back, where

Jivima had broken my bangles, I held on to my long braid. Ba followed close behind, holding a lantern.

"Leela, let it go," Bapuji said. His voice was firm.

A scream deep inside me turned into tears.

Kaki unbraided my hair. My eyes pleading, my lips trembling, I looked at Ba. When our eyes met, she looked away, focusing her gaze beyond the darkened horizon.

The morning was barely breaking when Nathu covered the ground with a piece of jute. I sat down on it, pulled my knees up to my chest, and wrapped my arms around my legs. Kaki sat on her knees in front of me, pressing her large palms on my shoulders while Nathu sat behind me. He took his scissors and cut as close to my head as he could, and my hair tumbled onto the ground in a heap. He swept it aside and shaved my scalp clean and shiny with a razor.

When I stood up, my head felt lighter. Was it because the weight of the hair was gone, or because I was going to faint? Ba and Kaki both reached out to me. I held on to them for support.

I stared at the heap of hair on the floor, knowing I would never again be able to wash it with *aritha* fruit until white foam covered every strand. I wouldn't be able to dry it in the gentle morning rays. Ba would never need to rub oil in my hair and braid it.

Just last year I'd learned to make a bun with the flick of my wrist. I'd practiced and practiced until it came out round and even each time. I'd learned for nothing.

The sun, soft as an angel, rose in the east as they walked me inside the house.

During the last nine days I'd cried enough to fill a well, and I'd shed my last tears this morning before everyone arrived. With a shaved head, there was no telling where my face stopped and my head started. I glanced at the mirror and saw that my forehead was as blank as a new slate. But it wasn't really brand new, and it wasn't blank. I knew one of the words for me was widhwa, but I knew many would call me *raand*. I despised it. Raand meant widow, but in a hateful, disgusting way. It was a swear word.

Why did kismet have to scribble such a terrible word on my forehead?

I took a bath after Nathu left. Ba handed me a sari to wear.

It was a *chidri*, a widow's sari, just like the one Jivima wore. On auspicious occasions women wearing chidri were to be avoided, for they'd bring bad luck. But weren't the women who wore them old and frail like Jivima, with wrinkled faces, stooped shoulders, and missing teeth? Were some of them young and I just hadn't noticed them? What about the two widows I had seen at the bonfire? They were like shadows. Was I going to become like them and melt into darkness?

I unfolded the chidri slowly. It had a strange smell—maybe of the cloth mill—and it felt stiff and rough under my fingers. We always bought good quality cotton that became softer after being washed, so I knew this would, too.

The chidri was the color of tobacco with a little vermilion thrown in, more brown than red. There were small white flowers scattered all over it. I knew that it wouldn't be long before the brown-red would bleed and wilt the white blossoms away.

Kaki came in the room and saw me staring at it. "Let me help you," she said, and began tucking the chidri into my petticoat. If that was the only help she could give me, there was no more hope. The fabric scratched my stomach. I wanted to tear it off and fling it far away. But people would be arriving soon, and I had to be ready for the role that had been handed to me by my karma. And there was no escaping one's karma.

But what kind of karma had merited this punishment?

The ninth day was the most important day after a death. People began arriving soon after breakfast.

Bapuji and Lakha put several khatlis covered with blankets under the shade of the kesuda tree.

When relatives arrived, the older men sat on khatlis, smoking *bidis* and whispering between each drag, while the younger men stood or squatted on the ground. The women filled the corridor that surrounded three sides of our house. There was too much grief and too much mourning.

All of a sudden, I heard a screaming cry. It was Masi. She entered the house sobbing wildly and banging her hands against her chest. It was as if she'd just heard the news of Ramanlal's death and had come for the first time to express her grief. It was customary to cry and beat your bosom to show your sorrow. Masi was very good at it, and that day she showed the world that she was shattered by Ramanlal's death.

For the past nine days she'd come every single day, but today she grabbed me, took me in her lap, and held me tightly. Her wailing was punctured by her words. "What a sky of grief has fallen on my Leela! What calamity has befallen my sister!" I tried to wiggle away, but Masi had a python's grip even in her show of despair.

Two more women came in crying and banging their chests, and I managed to slip out of Masi's lap and scoot away to a corner, where I watched the women around me. Whenever new visitors entered, they'd cry with

Kaki and Ba for a while, and then it would quiet down. Between the sobs and tears they talked in hushed tones. All the women were wearing black and mumbling that Ramanlal's death had made my happiness disappear like burning camphor.

Masi tucked her hair behind her ear. "How's my sister to bear such a heavy load? To have a widowed daughter in her house is like having an elephant's foot on her chest. Who knows what will happen when Leela's older? She's the youngest, so she's more than a little spoiled and sharp as a bull's horns. She won't listen to her ba, and she'll disgrace the family. I don't have a daughter, but if I did and if she were widowed, I'd not let her wander off even as far as the end of my sari. I shudder at the thought of the coming days. When Leela's beauty blossoms, what will happen? She'll be as wild as a kothimda vine in monsoon."

"Don't you worry," Jivima said. Her hand trembled as she put it on Masi's shoulder. "Don't forget that sense arrives before beauty. God gives sense at sixteen and beauty at twenty for a reason. Leela will have time enough to tame her mind so her beauty will not become a burden."

If Masi were truly worried about me, then she should talk to Ba privately. My family spoiled me with *things*, but I wasn't wild. I would never shame them.

Just then more women entered, crying loudly. If Masi said anything else, her words were buried under their grief.

The courtyard was pumped with breaths of tobacco. Through the smoky haze the men's white and black turbans looked like giant baskets full of cracked shingoda fruit, white flesh surrounded by waxy, black skin.

The sky turned bright and the air was warm. Our house and yard were full of people, but I was still waiting for Kanubhai and my cousin Jaya. I cupped my hand over my eyes and looked beyond the front door and the yard toward the dusty street, but I couldn't see a cart for as far as my vision could stretch.

A few minutes later I heard the sound of the bells tied around the bullocks' necks before I even saw them stop in front of our gate. My heart jumped. It was my cousin Jaya! In the past I would have ran and told her all the gossip I'd heard before she'd even stepped through the door. Instead, like a proper widow, I had to sit and wait for her to come to me.

Jaya wore a black sari with a blue pattern that framed her oval face and wide, almond eyes. Her forehead was brightened by a red chandlo. The round pendant of her gold necklace was cradled in the hollow of her neck. I had seen her last year at her anu, and since then she'd grown taller and her lips and cheeks had a rounded, full-moon look. Jaya must be happy with her husband and his family, I thought.

How our lives had changed. What would have happened if Ramanlal had lived and Jaya's husband had died? Then she'd be sitting in my place and I'd be in hers. For a moment, my mind was caught in a storm. *What if? What if?* was all I could hear. I pulled my chidri snug around me as if I could muffle the thoughts with the coarse fabric.

Jaya rushed toward me and knelt at my side. I threw myself into her arms. "Jaya, what am I going to do? I'll go crazy."

"No you won't. I'll be here. We'll talk when we're alone," she said, and held me for a long time.

Later, when Jaya got up to serve water to the visitors, I heard the laughter of children playing outside in the street. I could imagine them running around raising dust, and I could nearly feel my bare feet dancing on the street. I moved closer to the window.

Kaki had gone into the kitchen, and everyone else was deep in conversation. No one was paying attention to me, so I climbed up on the iron barrel that contained our yearly supply of castor oil–coated wheat. Through the round window, I saw a girl with a braid swinging on each side of her big ears. She was playing tag in the street with the other children. The girl was only a few years younger than me.

Jaya tapped my shoulder. "Get down. You have to behave properly when people are watching you."

I turned to her, and she took both my hands and helped me down.

When the brass bells rang out from Lord Rama's Temple, marking the afternoon prayer, the dark-clothed women rose. They all moved at the same time, like a giant herd of black water buffalo. It was time to go to Ramanlal's house for the ceremony.

The men walked ahead and the women followed them. Tomorrow or the day after or next month, I thought, things will change for *them*. After the mourning period, the men would wrap their heads in colorful turbans laced with gold and silver thread. The women would wear saris in shades of eggplant and lime, their bracelets would tinkle and their nose rings would sparkle. Their hearts would be filled with happiness at festivals, weddings, and celebrations. I would be shunned from all that. I could never be joyful again.

Just as all the people moved out of the front courtyard, my brother, Kanubhai, came in. He had to lean down to avoid bumping his head on the gate. He was taller than Bapuji, Kaka, and most of the men in Jamlee. We met him at the door as we were about to follow the other people to Ramanlal's house. His face was as bright as if he had run a mile. He saw me and gasped. The color from his face drained away. "Ba, Kaki, what have you done to Leela? She is . . . she is just a child! Did you have to shave her head?"

"You know we had to," Ba said.

"I know it is custom, but you don't have to follow it. This is a crime!" His voice was loud, and some women turned their heads to see what was happening.

Ba put her finger on her mouth. "Don't make a scene now. Keep your lips tightly together until we return home. If we want to live in society, we have to follow its rules."

"And if we don't? What will people do? Throw us out of the caste? Let them." He was shaking.

"Then it will be living death. We will be shunned. We won't even be able to find four men to carry us to the cremation ground when we die," Kaki said.

"So we sacrifice Leela?" he yelled. Now even the men turned around to see what was happening.

"For everyone's sake, wait until we return home," Kaki said. He grit his teeth as if to seal his lips.

Ba pointed toward the group of men walking ahead of the women. "Hurry, go with your bapuji and kaka. They need you now."

"No one needs me more than Leela. I'll walk with her." He took my hand in his. "I am so sorry that you have to go through this, this—" His voice ripped before he could finish.

I pressed his firm fingers, trying to gain as much strength from them as I could. I wished he would just stay here by my side. If he and Jaya were with me, I'd be able to endure widowhood. "Help me," I whispered.

"I will," he replied, squeezing my hand.

When we got to Ramanlal's house, Fat Soma came rushing to Kanubhai. Ba grabbed hold of my hand. "You can't go with Kanubhai or Fat Soma. Come with me."

I sat between Ba and Kaki. Other women surrounded us. Ramanlal's ba's eyes were red and puffy like Ba's. They looked so sad, I avoided meeting them. The ceremony started and the priest recited from the *Bhagavad Gita*, "'The soul is neither born nor does it die at any time. It is unborn, imperishable, and timeless.'"

We were followers of *Sanatan Dharma*, the eternal law. What the priest said was the highest truth for us, and our daily lives and actions were to be conducted with this law in mind. According to our religion, only Ramanlal's body was gone. If his soul was everlasting, why did I have to be punished?

The priest went on chanting. His voice was even and soothing, and I became drowsy. I must have nearly dozed off, because Ba nudged me once.

After we returned home I wanted to talk to Kanubhai, but he, Bapuji, and Kaka went into Kaka's room and closed the door. Ba, Kaki, Jaya, and I sat in the chauk. I was so tired, I rested my head against Jaya's shoulder. Someone must have slipped a pillow under my head and spread my silk blanket over me, because that is how I woke up.

"You slept for a long time," Jaya said. She was sitting by me, reading a book.

I looked up at the sky and saw that the sun had dipped behind the *jamboo* tree. I took off my blanket and folded it. I glanced at Kaka's room. The door was open, but no one was in there.

"Where is Kanubhai, Jaya?" I asked.

She shook her head. "He's gone."

"Gone where?"

Jaya wiped a tear from her eye. "Back to Ahmedabad. I . . . I tried to stop him but couldn't."

"But I thought he would stay." A dreadful fear gripped me. Kanubhai must have fought with Bapuji and Kaka. Did they get mad and ask him to leave the house? What if they told him not to come back? "Did they raise their voices?" I asked Jaya.

"They talked for a long time, but I couldn't hear anything."

{ 71 }

Jaya pulled out a piece of paper from her poulka pocket. "Before he left he gave me a message to give you."

I unfolded the paper and read.

Leela, my dearest sister,
I had to leave because of an argument with Bapuji. It is bad enough that Ramanlal has died, but I don't understand why you have to cut your hair and wear a chidri. I tried to reason with Bapuji, but he wouldn't listen. He thinks my mind is polluted with new ideas and that I have no respect for tradition. There are no words to describe how sad and outraged I am.

I promise to help you get out of this misery. I'll be back soon.

Your brother

I handed the note to Jaya. After she was done reading it, she said, "I wish he could've taken you with him."

I whispered, "I don't know when Kanubhai is going to come back. When he does, though, I'll be here, keeping corner."

I could feel the blood drain out of my face. My heart turned numb.

SIX

OUR HOUSE had lost its happiness and there was nothing we could do to bring it back. Every time Ba looked at me she started crying. Kaki stayed in the kitchen but cooked little and served food silently. Every morning she prayed for a long time, and I wondered what she could be praying for. She and God couldn't change anything, could they?

Bapuji and Kaka went to the farm and watered the winter wheat to keep it alive. I don't know how much it helped the crop, but it got them out of the house. At home they moved like shadows. Kaka used to take so much pride in tying his turban so that the twists of the bends lined up perfectly. Now his turban was scrunched up and flat on top. Bapuji's eyes were dull and listless and had sunk deeper into his face. His shoulders stooped like he was carrying a bale of hay.

We hadn't heard from Kanubhai. Didn't he know I needed him? It felt like our family had died with Ramanlal.

Jaya stayed by me as if she were afraid I'd get lost. We slept on a mattress spread out on the chauk floor. In the morning she'd wait for me to wake before she got out of bed. Sitting side by side on the back patio, we would chew on our acacia sticks, and after we were done brushing our teeth with them she'd make tea for us.

Jaya would read me the newspaper after breakfast. Most of the time the words hit my ears but didn't sink into my head.

One day Jaya picked up the paper. I watched her face turn glum as her eyes scanned the words.

"What happened?" I asked.

She raised her hand, gesturing at me to be silent. When she was done reading, she took a deep breath. "Gandhiji is on a hunger strike until the mill owners and the mill workers settle their dispute."

I remembered reading that the mill workers wanted a pay raise that the mill owners didn't want to give. "I don't see why that would make any difference to the mill owners. They're rich. Why should they care if Gandhiji eats or not?"

"Because Gandhiji is a family friend of the mill

owners. They love him. They wouldn't want him to go without food."

Gandhiji was not a mill worker or a mill owner. I was puzzled as to why he would risk his health and life for other people. Jaya looked worried, though, so I didn't ask her any more questions.

That afternoon when Masi, Jivima, Heeraben, and other neighbors had gathered in the front corridor, Jaya asked if I wanted to visit with them.

I shook my head. I didn't want to see anyone except my family.

"It might help," Jaya said.

"How can it help? I've heard them whisper about how ugly I look without my hair. You can just go if you don't want to be with me." I was sorry as soon as I said that. Jaya had been like my own shadow, and now I was resentful. If she was hurt by my anger, she didn't show it.

"Do you want to stay in the room and read *Mahabharat*?" she asked.

Mahabharat was the epic story of the struggle between cousins of an ancient dynasty. On one side there were five virtuous brothers, called the Pandavas, and on the other side there were one hundred greedy brothers, called the Kauravas. Kaki had told me the story many times before, but I'd never read it. The story was long and the book was heavy. Jaya put the book on a wooden stand. She and I sat cross-legged on the floor in front of it.

Every afternoon Jaya would read a few pages to me. When she got tired I'd take over. My favorite person in the story was the second Pandava brother, Bheem. He had amazing strength, and the Kauravas were afraid of him. One day the Kauravas teased Bheem and then they climbed up a tree, knowing Bheem was too big to chase them into the canopy. Bheem was smart, though. He put his arm around the trunk and shook it so hard that the Kauravas fell out of the tree, one by one.

The thought of a hundred evil brothers dropping like fruit made me and Jaya laugh out loud. I laughed so hard that for a while it was just me, Jaya, and the story. Then, before I knew it, my laughter had turned into sobs. "Widowhood is going to be with me for as long as I live, isn't it?" I blurted.

Jaya eyes filled with sadness. I rested my head on her shoulder and began playing with her hair. "I miss my hair," I said.

"You can comb mine."

I looked up at her. "Do you think I can grow my hair again one day?"

"I'm not sure."

I stared at the book. The lines on the page seemed

to merge together. "Gandhiji has written many articles about how women and untouchables have been treated badly in our society," Jaya whispered. "It's in the newspaper and people are talking about it. Our country is changing. People might give up their old ways. Maybe—"

I sat up straight. "Gandhiji can keep on writing, but do you think anyone cares about being fair? Look at me. If they did, I wouldn't be sitting in a corner with a shaved head, wearing a chidri."

"Oh, Leela!" She put her hand on my shoulder.

"Nothing will ever change in Jamlee," I said.

"Remember a few days ago, when Gandhiji started his fast, you didn't think the mill owners would budge, but they did. They gave the workers a raise."

"That's different. Gandhiji is a politician. Politicians can help poor workers, but how can they help me? They can negotiate with mill owners, but how can they negotiate with the people in Jamlee? Kanubhai fought with Bapuji because of me. If Bapuji won't listen to his own son, why would he listen to a stranger like Gandhiji?"

Jaya's brows tensed. "I'm not sure."

I shook my head. "A miracle is what I need," I mumbled, and started reading *Mahabharat* again. There were many miracles in it.

Three weeks had gone by since Jaya had come, and now it was time for her to go home. The day before she left, a letter from Kanubhai came, but it wasn't for me. That night in bed, I asked Jaya, "Do you know what Kanubhai wrote?"

She turned on her side and faced me. "Not a word."

"Why are they keeping it a secret?"

"Don't worry. I'm sure he'll write to you soon."

"Do you have to go?" I asked.

She touched my shoulder. "I do."

I couldn't imagine my days without Jaya. How would I spend my afternoons? Who would I talk to? "Can you come back soon?" I asked her.

She shook her head.

A lump rose up from nowhere and settled in my throat. I lay there thinking about the summers Jaya had come with her mother, bapuji and Kaka's sister. Jaya and I had jumped rope, played hopscotch, and gone to temple. All year, I was jealous of other girls who had so many brothers and sisters to play with, but my envy melted when Jaya came.

In the afternoon, when all the adults napped, Kanubhai would read a book and Jaya would braid my hair, or we would pluck *mehndi* leaves and grind them on a washing stone under the shade of a jamboo tree until our hands turned red. Sometimes she would tell me a story, or we would take out Ba's and Kaki's old saris and hang them up in the corridor and transform it into a little room. Then we would take out my tiny brass pots and pans and play house-house in it. Now I wished I could have Jaya for a few more months, but she was a married woman and had responsibilities. Her sister-in-law was heavy with child, and Jaya had to return to her family.

The lump in my throat turned to tears, and I cried softly.

"Leela, I wish I could stay for the whole year," Jaya whispered.

I knew Jaya wasn't just saying that. She would have if she could. I pulled my blanket all the way up to my chin, even though the night was warm and the chauk's stone floor was releasing the heat it had captured from the midday sun. "Once you leave, who will I talk to? What will I do?"

Tears began to well up again.

She squeezed my shoulder. "Your masi calls you spoiled for a reason. It is because you always get what you want. Now is the time to be stubborn. Fight."

"I'll try. Without you, it'll be hard. I'll miss you."

She kissed my cheek. "And I'll miss you."

Right above me was the cluster of seven stars called

Saptarshi, named after the seven *rishis*, wise men, who had lived a long time ago. I asked them for courage, guidance, and blessings. I knew their blessings could make a lion as docile as a cow and reverse the flow of a river. Maybe they could change a widow's life.

Kaki had told me the story of Markand, a child who was born when the rishis were alive. He was not expected to live beyond five years. Whenever Markand saw a rishi, he would join his hands and bow low with respect. Invariably the rishi would give him a blessing of long life. Over the years, Markand received blessings from so many great rishis that it's said he lives forever.

"Jaya," I whispered, "do you think Saptarshi would bless me from such a distance?"

Instead of answering, Jaya turned on her left side and mumbled, "Saptarshi, Saptarshi."

I watched her hair and earring swathed in the moonlight. Her breathing slowed. Only the wind heard my words.

Jaya left in a bullock cart early the next morning. Even in mourning Jaya couldn't wear black to go back to her husband, because it was a color of bad luck and death. So she wore a white sari with a blue border. Ba tucked an old piece of cloth around Jaya's sari to keep it clean during the ride.

The house felt as quiet as a cremation ground after Jaya left. Since we were in mourning, we couldn't celebrate any holidays or attend weddings or janoi celebrations. Each new day was the same as the day before. Just thinking about it was suffocating. It had only been a month since I'd become a widow, and I still had eleven months to keep corner.

I was a widow and was expected to behave like one. If the changes Jaya spoke of were really happening, then like rain transforming the earth from brown to green, my life could change. I didn't think so, but I hoped.

SEVEN

WHEN I WOKE UP the next morning, the first thing I thought was: a month ago today Ramanlal was bitten by a snake. I tried to push it out of my mind, but it stayed there like a bell tied around a bullock's neck. I knew it would keep ringing all day.

Kaki was perspiring heavily when she returned from the well. She said that the sun had sucked up the water, and the water level was so low that instead of two pots of drinking and cooking water, she only got one. I watched from the window as the kesuda tree shed its shriveled-up blossoms. The two hottest months, April and May, were still ahead of us before monsoon season arrived, and I wondered what we would do if the well went dry.

It was time to pay taxes on last year's crop, but because of the drought, some of the farmers from our

Kheda district didn't have any money. Gandhiji had asked the sarkar to waive the taxes, but they refused. One of the farmers in a neighboring town had committed suicide because he couldn't pay the taxes. The news had spread quickly, and in the evening, farmers from Jamlee gathered under our kesuda tree. Unlike other nights, they hardly talked, and when they did, their voices were muffled.

A couple of nights later, while Ba and I were washing dishes, Bapuji came and said, "Gandhiji is coming to Nadiad the day after tomorrow to talk to the farmers. I am going."

Bapuji didn't usually go to Nadiad without a reason. It seemed like a long way to travel for a few words. "Just to listen to him?" I asked, rinsing a plate.

"Yes," he said, lifting his heavy eyebrows and folding his hands in front of him.

"The British sarkar is strong willed, so nothing will come of this, but I suppose you have to go to show your support," Ba said. She took the plate from my hand and wiped it. "Be careful. Too many agitated men are like wild bulls. It doesn't take much for them to turn violent."

"I'll be careful," he replied.

* * *

Bapuji went to Nadiad the next day. I read the newspaper to see if I could find out how the meeting was going. The trouble with the paper was that news always came after things happened, so for a day or two I wouldn't know anything. By that time Bapuji would be home anyway.

When Bapuji returned, there was a glimmer in his eyes and a bounce in his walk that I hadn't seen since I had become a widow. He told us about the meeting while we drank afternoon tea. "Farmers from all over the Kheda district came to listen to Gandhiji. There were thousands of us."

"Thousands!" Ba gasped.

I tried to imagine so many people in one place.

Bapuji cleared his throat. "Yes. Gandhiji made it clear to us that what the sarkar is doing is wrong, and our only course is *satyagrah*."

I had never heard the word *satyagrah*. "What does that mean?"

"*Satya* means truth, and *agrah* mean insistence. Gandhiji believes that if we use the force of truth we can fight injustice. He named the movement satyagrah."

"How can you fight with truth? People fight with swords, or guns."

"Gandhiji has made it his weapon. The sarkar insists on collecting taxes even after our crops failed.

The truth is we can't pay because we didn't make any money, so Gandhiji is asking us to unite and oppose the sarkar. This will be the first act of satyagrah in Kheda. More than a thousand of us have taken a pledge not to pay a single rupee in taxes. And I won't pay, no matter what happens."

Bapuji and other farmers like him had fallen in love with satyagrah, but wouldn't the Engrej get angry? And if they did, what would we do? Whenever someone resisted the sarkar, they had their army beat him up and throw him in jail. It had happened many times before and could certainly happen again.

"You will disobey the sarkar?" I could feel the fear lurking in my words.

"O, Rama," Kaka called out as he got up. "Do what you think is right," he said to Bapuji, then he turned and went to his room. A few moments later I heard tanpura music. Before I became a widow, he used to play it once or twice a week, and always at night. Now he hardly talked to the men who gathered in our compound under the kesuda tree, but played the tanpura and sang instead. Today he had picked it up in the afternoon. I didn't like that he played music and sang devotional songs alone in his room. It seemed as if he had lost interest in our family. I wondered if Kaki would notice and say something to him.

When the men gathered in our courtyard that evening, I caught the thread of their talks. Their voices were strong but even, and the words like satyagrah, Gandhiji, Kheda, drought, sarkar, mercy, and pledge whirled in the air.

The hot afternoons were longer and quieter than the nights. When the darkness came, I expected silence so I could go to sleep, but when the day was young, there was an unbearable stillness that lurked behind every door. Ba, Bapuji, Kaka, and Kaki took long naps, birds hid in their nests, and dogs didn't bark.

I sat in the corner of our lobby and wondered what I was going to do for eleven more months. Sometimes my hand would reach behind my ear to twirl a lock of hair that wasn't there. Sometimes I would open the wooden cupboard and take out my ghagri-poulka sets and stare at them. If Ramanlal were alive, I'd be getting ready for my anu. His ba would have bought me a shimmering sari. I might have helped his grandmother make pickles. But the reality was: I was bald, I only wore chidri, and I had nowhere to go. For me, time burned away slow as dried cow dung.

I thought about how strongly Bapuji felt about satyagrah. It made me wonder. If Bapuji was for truth and fairness, then he should know that what was happening to me wasn't fair. Why didn't he fight for me?

One day, Saviben, the principal of my school, came to our house. I hadn't been to school or seen any of my classmates for the past month, and it felt like someone from a dream was visiting me. When school started last year, I had four friends in my class. Two of them had their anu before *Holi* and had left Jamlee. One girl's mother was always sick, and she was absent most of the time, which left only Tara, who was blind.

Saviben had gone to college to become a teacher. When she was working in a school in Nadiad, one of the British education inspectors who met her had been so impressed that Saviben had increased the girls' enrollment at the school that she recommended Saviben for the principal post in Jamlee. The streets had been swept and sprinkled with water on the day Saviben became principal because the Engrej lady had come to attend the ceremony, too.

When I saw Saviben for the first time, I had been surprised by her delicate oval face, small mouth, and youthful looks. Her nose was slim, straight, and rather long, with a gold ring nestled on the right side. The women all talked about how fashionable and modern Saviben was to wear the *palav*, the end of her sari, draped over her left shoulder. The loose end sashayed when she walked. Women of Jamlee wore their palav over their right shoulder and tucked part of the loose end in. Today Saviben wore an earth-colored sari with a seashell print.

After expressing her sorrow over my misfortune, Saviben asked Ba what she was going to do about my studies.

"She has to keep corner for many months yet," Ba told her.

"I understand. I can come here three times a week and work with her."

Ba sighed. "What's the use?"

"Times are changing now. Leela can use an education."

"We're not dead," Ba said. Her voice was sickle sharp.

I looked at Saviben. If she was offended by Ba's words, she didn't show it. Instead she gave me a smile, and her teeth, each one as perfectly shaped as a pomegranate seed, gleamed.

Kaki was quietly measuring out her tobacco and didn't say a word. I twisted the end of my chidri.

"I'm sure Leela doesn't need money to support herself, but it wouldn't do her any harm to finish school. It would occupy her time, too."

I had never thought much about studying. Why should I? I was going to have my anu and then I would stay home to care for my husband and family. Now that

I was a widow I wouldn't be doing that. If Ba agreed with Saviben, then I'd have to keep going to school. I didn't want to be a scholar.

Saviben looked at me. I avoided her gaze and looked down. She spoke slowly but firmly. "Because Leela attended classes up until a few weeks ago, I'll promote her to the next standard even if she doesn't take her final exams. But only if she resumes her studies."

Ba sighed. "Maybe after Leela is done keeping corner."

"She'll fall behind sitting at home for that long a time."

"It's kind of you to offer to come to our house," Kaki said, and gave me a commanding look, adding, "Leela will work hard and make you proud."

Saviben glanced at Ba. I knew that once Kaki made the decision, Ba wouldn't argue. Kaki was older. Ba nodded in approval.

Even though I didn't care if I studied or not, it was decided for me. I was going to continue.

EIGHT

O N T H E M O R N I N G of my first lesson,
Kaki opened the drawing room. "You should sit here
when Saviben comes."

"In this room?" I could taste the spice of surprise in
my voice.

The drawing room stayed closed most of the time,
except when important visitors came. Why was Kaki
asking me to sit on the hand-painted wooden couch
with the plump seats and soft pillows? The pillows
were stuffed with the cotton of a *shimla* tree—cotton
fluffier than a fool's thought. Unlike the rough stone
floor of the chauk, or the mud floor of the corridor, the
floor of the drawing room was covered with tiles and
felt smooth and cool, like a freshly made bed on a winter night. Was a widow allowed to be so indulgent?

"I want you to concentrate on your studies. Learn as

much as you can from your *guru*. Remember, she deserves the utmost respect."

"Yes," I replied.

I could not settle down. I darted in and out of the room, bringing my slate and books, bringing a small brass pot of water for us, straightening the sheets on the couch, dusting the table again and again. This was the first time someone was coming for me and no one else. And it was the first time the drawing room was opened up just for me and my teacher.

Ba was peeling sweet potatoes in the kitchen. I pulled her hand. "Come, see where Saviben and I are going to sit."

When Ba saw the door to the drawing room open, she looked at Kaki in surprise.

"Leela and her teacher need privacy. There are too many visitors and too much commotion in the corridor," Kaki explained.

Ba put her hand on my shoulder. "Make the best use of your time with Saviben."

Ba looked at me with such expectation that I said, "I will, Ba," even though I had not given it much thought.

I sat in the drawing room, looking out the window, waiting for Saviben. Last year when she became our principal, she was dressed in an eggplant-colored sari with golden stars embroidered all over it. I called it the *nisha-*

akash sari, the night-sky sari. She spoke only a few words that day, but I remembered her saying, "It is not too far in the future when a woman will walk with a man and become his true partner." Then she pointed at the handful of us and said, "And you are the girls who will do it."

I didn't understand what she meant by "true partner," yet there was something in her voice and eyes that made her words stay with me.

When I saw Saviben walking through the front courtyard, without thinking, I clasped my hands together and said a prayer to Lord Ganesh to remove obstacles from my path.

Saviben started with math. She gave me some multiplication and long division, and while I worked on it she wrote out problems in a notebook for homework. As I worked, the excitement from the morning vanished, and I wondered if it was better to sit alone in a corner or to churn your brain with 32,456 divided by 24.

As I handed Saviben my slate to check the answers, I noticed her sari palav was touching me. I traced the printed dark green leaves and clusters of purple fruit on her silver cotton sari with my index finger.

I was engrossed in tracing the pattern until she said, "Leela," and tugged the sari back gently.

I didn't realize I'd covered my lap with her palav.

"I . . . I didn't mean to. . . ."

"It's all right."

Out of ten problems, I got three wrong.

After Saviben left, Ba and Kaki asked how I did. "Not good," I replied.

I had almost two full days to do my homework, but I pushed it off until the last minute. That morning I raced through the math problems and skimmed pages of the history chapter Saviben had assigned. I finished just before she walked in.

Today her sari was the color of evening pink, the last splash of color scattered by the setting sun. It made my chidri look even more dull and lifeless. I tried to keep my hands away from her sari while she checked my math.

When I found out I had done half of the math problems wrong, I was so ashamed that I couldn't even look at Saviben when she explained them to me. I had made some really careless mistakes. In one place I had written 4 x 2 = 6!

When she quizzed me about the history lessons she had assigned me, I didn't know the answers. I felt my face burning as I fumbled. It's one thing to be in a class and to get one question wrong, but it is another to be sitting with your principal all by yourself and come out looking so *buddhu*, dumb. I wished Saviben hadn't come to teach me. I had no use for all this math and history.

My widowed life didn't need either one of them. Then I thought, if I don't pay attention and learn, there will be nothing for me to do at all.

"Let's do poetry today," Saviben said, opening a book she had brought with her.

I read the poem, but I was quiet when she asked me what I thought of it.

"Tell me what it says. Don't be afraid. There's no right or wrong answer."

I told her what I thought, and she listened without interrupting. Then she told me her impression of the poem. We read a few more poems and discussed them.

Reading poetry was easier than doing math. I found poetry soothing, while numbers did somersaults in my head and confused me.

Then Saviben asked me to fetch the newspaper. I hadn't looked at one since Bapuji had gone to Nadiad. I brought the paper and tried to hand it to Saviben.

"I want you to read it to me. Stop and ask if you have questions."

Why was she making me do this? I knew this wasn't schoolwork, because we'd never had to do this in school. But out of respect for her, I read the headline from the front page, "Kheda satyagrah continues. Four thousand gather in Borsad."

There was a picture of Gandhiji dressed in a small white cap, undershirt, and white dhoti, speaking in front of a large gathering.

Kaki once showed me a picture of Gandhiji she had cut from the front page of the *Mumbai Samachar*. At that time he was dressed in *angarkha*, a long white shirt, and a dhoti. His white turban had covered part of his forehead and eyebrow. His mustache was thick, and he had Buddha's long ears. His eyes were dark. Except for his deep, steady gaze, he was like Bapuji or any other Gujarati man from our community.

"Why doesn't he wear a turban and angarkha like he used to?" I asked.

"He wants to dress like his fellow countrymen."

"But he's a lawyer. Shouldn't he dress properly?"

"Do you think how a person dresses always reflects who they are?"

I glanced at my chidri and shook my head.

She continued. "Besides, Gandhiji wants to help the poor; if he's dressed like the poor, it will help him gain their trust and support."

"Bapuji went to hear Gandhiji in Nadiad and joined the satyagrah. He's not going to pay the taxes, even though he can afford to," I said.

"Do you think he should?"

How should I know what he should do? I had only

lived thirteen years. This was something Bapuji and Kaka had to decide. "I don't know."

Saviben put her arm around my shoulder. "You're not the only one who isn't sure. Satyagrah isn't easy. It requires self-discipline and unity."

I remembered Gandhiji going on a fast for the mill workers. It must have been hard to go hungry. "Do you think Bapuji and the farmers will have to fast?"

"I don't think so, but that doesn't mean there won't be any hardships. For breaking the law, the sarkar can take farmers' land, drive them out of their homes, and throw them in jail."

"In jail!" A wave of fear rippled through my heart. I hadn't thought about it since Bapuji went to Nadiad. Now that Saviben mentioned it, I realized that the sarkar *could* put people in jail to show its authority. I became convinced that the sarkar was going to lock Bapuji up. Soon. "Then, I don't understand why Bapuji has pledged satyagrah. We have money. He should pay the taxes."

"And not worry about the others?"

I didn't answer and looked at the floor.

"What if your family were poor?" she asked. I didn't lift my eyes. "You know the saying, 'A stick is a stick until many come together.' Then they can become as strong as a log. If people unite for one cause, then the

British will have to listen. They can't put everyone in jail," Saviben said.

I nodded. I understood what she was saying, but I was still worried about Bapuji.

The word *satyagrah* spun in my head that night. The idea of truth was supposed to be good and pure, but I was scared of its consequences.

Saviben had asked me to read the newspaper and write about what I read for homework. She also told me to read more poems and to write one if I wanted.

News of farmers joining Gandhiji remained on the front page over the next few days. He had traveled to Ahmedabad, Nadiad, and even to Mumbai to gain support for Kheda farmers. He had met the British commissioner and revenue board members in Ahmedabad regarding the drought. I hoped this would have a happy ending, like the mill workers' dispute, but I wasn't sure. The sarkar was not going to give up.

I read the newspaper, wrote a short report about it, and at the end added, "I hope Gandhiji's negotiations will be successful." I read a few poems but couldn't write one. I didn't know what to say in a poem, or how to say it.

I had been studying with Saviben for two weeks when I received a short letter from Kanubhai. It said:

Dear Leela,

I hope this letter finds you in good health. How do you like studying with your principal? Are you working hard and learning a lot? Keep up your work so you can take your finals next year.

I will try to come back before the mangoes ripen. Don't eat my share!

Your brother

Had Bapuji written to Kanubhai that Saviben was teaching me?

The heat of April was unbearable, and I used a bamboo fan to stay cool. When Saviben came, I gave her one, too. One day Saviben wore a sari that was cats'-eye yellow, with wild grass printed around the edge. Her palav cascaded from her left shoulder onto the couch we were sitting on. Unlike the rest of the sari, the palav was woven in shades of green and looked like the edge of a jungle.

Saviben caught me staring at her sari. "What are you thinking?" she asked.

"Nothing. I mean, if you look at your palav long enough, you might see a lion hiding in there."

She laughed. "I never thought of it. But you're right. You might." Then she whispered softly, "I know you miss wearing colors. Let's pretend that all the saris I wear are yours. That way you can touch them as much as you want to. Tell me what color sari I should wear next time?"

"Soft green."

The following Monday, Saviben was dressed in pistachio-colored silk. Her saris became our routine, our game, our secret. Sometimes she spread the palav on my lap, covering my chidri. For a while at least, the green of the monsoon earth or the purple of jamboo fruit covered me. While I studied, I pretended I wasn't a widow. I didn't always tell Saviben the colors I wanted her to wear. Sometimes I wanted to be surprised.

One day I spread Saviben's gold-and-green palav on my lap. While I was reading, I saw Masi poke her head into the drawing room, but I didn't think much about it. Later that evening I heard her talking to Ba.

"If Leela were my daughter, I wouldn't allow her to study with Saviben. She's a modern woman with ideas more twisted than a ginger root."

"What do you mean?"

"Have you seen how she lets Leela cover her chidri with her palav? Today she will tempt Leela with her sari, tomorrow it could be more. Why is she doing this, I ask? Shouldn't she do her work and go on her own way? Don't you see she's influencing Leela?"

"She's Leela's teacher."

"Yes. She should teach Leela how to read and count, but she mustn't spoil her with modern thoughts and modern ideas. Leela is a widow and must live like one. As time goes by, Saviben might tell Leela that she shouldn't cut her hair, she should throw away her chidri, and even wear bangles! If Leela doesn't develop self-discipline, how will she protect herself from bigger temptations?"

When I heard the words *self-discipline*, I thought of my conversation with Saviben about satyagrah. I wanted to tell Masi that I could learn self-control by joining the satyagrah. My words would have ignited her and she'd have burned up like a dry stick, so I didn't. I knew what Masi meant. She wanted me to have the will power to resist men and protect my widowhood. She'd mentioned this more than once, and I was getting tired of it.

Masi waited for Ba to reply, but Ba was silent. "This whole matter is ripe with bad omens," Masi said before she left.

On the day of my wedding anniversary, I thought about what I'd be doing if Ramanlal were alive. I'd be dressed in new clothes and the bangles I had bought at the fair; Ba would have tied silky strings with tassels at the end of my hair and put a black dot on my temple to ward off the evil eye. Now I knew the black dot didn't work; otherwise I wouldn't be a widow.

All day I thought about my wedding-day festivities, when I was nine: how Ramanlal and I had eaten sweet kansar, how my sari had sparkled, how the scent of flowers surrounded me.

That evening while Ba and Kaki were visiting a sick relative, I went to the cupboard and took out a red-and-white sari, which was hand woven with alternate threads of muslin and silk with a gold border. It was folded in a perfect square. Ba had worn that sari for her wedding, and then I had worn it for my wedding four years ago.

I opened up one fold and then another and then the third, until it was all one long piece flowing through my hands and falling like a stream onto the floor. I couldn't resist its festive colors and petal-soft touch. Flinging my chidri away, I wrapped the sandalwood-scented wedding sari around my waist once, then made a few pleats and tucked them in my petticoat and brought the loose end around my back and over from my shoulder to the front, covering my head.

I looked in the mirror again. It had been a long time since I'd seen myself in anything but a muddy-brown chidri. The red-and-white sari hypnotized me. There was still something missing. I took two silver boxes from the shelf. The first one contained kohl. I dipped my first finger in it, then applied it to my eyes. I moved my hand to my head to remove the remaining kohl from my finger by wiping it off onto my hair. I couldn't, so I used the end of the discarded chidri to clean my finger.

I opened the second silver box. I dipped the tip of my ring finger in the vermilion powder and touched it to the middle of my forehead, making a chandlo. The red of my chandlo and the red of the sari matched perfectly. I was so engrossed in admiring myself in the mirror that I didn't hear the latch of the front gate open or the approaching footsteps.

And then the whole Mahabharat started, a long battle of epic proportion that turned family members into enemies.

"What have you done, Leela? Don't you know that your husband is dead and you are a widhwa?" Masi shouted. Being sisters, Ba's and Masi's voices were similar, but the words that came out of their mouths were as different as soothing rain and pelting hail.

In the mirror I saw Masi's narrowed eyes focusing on me. Before I could turn to face her, she swooped like a vulture, grabbed my shoulders, jerked me around, and shook me. "Are your senses dulled and drowned? Has your brain dropped out of your skull? Why have you made such a show of yourself?"

The silver box fell. *Thup.*

I looked down. The brown floor was splashed with red. "Why don't you answer me? What kind of ghost is riding you?" Masi asked.

Masi was right. I had broken the rules of widowhood. Still, her malice angered me. "No ghost is riding me," I shouted.

"You . . . you tall as a nail! I am your masi. Don't talk back to me. Have you forgotten that you're a widow? Hear me, *raandi* raand! For this you'll be punished. I'll make sure of that."

I lifted my eyes and fixed them on Masi's face, my courage swelling from the word *raand.* If Masi had called me widhwa it would have been all right, but when she cursed me by calling me raand, it was as if she had sprayed me with filthy water.

"Don't just stand there as if your mouth is stitched tight. What could you have been thinking? You're old enough to understand that a widow must behave herself or she'll ruin her family's name. People will spit at you and shun you, and you'll put black marks on all of our faces," she said, smearing my chandlo with her palm.

"No! Don't touch me," I screamed, pushing her hand away. Masi's words stung, and my face burned with humiliation. Just because I was a widow didn't mean she could insult me and make me feel worthless.

Slowly, Masi walked backward, keeping her eyes on me. I didn't flinch. I answered her stare with my own. Then she stopped. "If Heeraben or Jivima or any of the other neighbors had found you like this, in two days the whole town would know, and then what would happen to our name, to our family honor?"

"I'm not your daughter. It's our name and our honor. Let it be muddied."

Masi stomped her foot, turned around, and marched out the door.

She'd come with her small brass pot to get buttermilk, but left without filling it.

That evening, Ba took the two silver boxes away and hid them.

"What you don't see, you don't seek. I've taken the wedding sari and your ghagri-poulka and stored them in the trunk under my bed," she said.

The wooden trunk was too heavy for me to pull out by myself. Those temptations were out of my reach.

I turned my face away.

NINE

O NE DAY, Saviben asked me to write down what had happened between her visits. That was part of my homework.

"I can't go out. Things happen *outside*, on the street, in school, at temple. What will I write?"

"Look closely. You'll find a lot going on in your own house and yard."

I couldn't tell Saviben that the only things that went on around this house were silence and grief. Our family didn't sing together anymore. Bapuji hardly talked, not even to scold me. Ba stared out the window and cried. Kaki never asked what I wanted to eat. For her, cooking had become a burden. Kaka and his tanpura made melancholy music. Lakha stayed busy with the animals and rarely showed his face. All this had drained out my heart as if it were a pot with a big hole. "Not in my yard. Not in this house," I replied.

"You know Tara. She's blind, but she sees with her ears, nose, and hands. You have an advantage over her."

I pictured Tara's fig-shaped face and blank eyes. "I don't have an advantage over Tara. She's free to see . . . I mean she can't see, but she doesn't have to keep corner. She's not a widow and never will be."

Saviben's forehead wrinkled. "I'm not sure I understand you."

Tara would forever remain blind, and I would forever remain a widow. The only difference was that people had not stolen Tara's eyesight, and if there were a way to restore it, some doctor would. But people had snatched my happiness and they were not going to give it back. In a way, Tara was luckier. "Tara is blind. No one will arrange her marriage and no one will marry her. And if she never marries, how can she ever be a widow? She'll never have to keep corner for a year, like I have to."

Saviben nodded.

I continued, "Ba tells me, 'Leela, a year is a sip of bitter *kadu* tea. You have no choice but to take it. You can sit and swoosh it around until your whole mouth tastes bitter, or you can swallow it quickly and move on to taste other things.' But kadu is for my own good. Kaki says it keeps me healthy. What does a year at home do?"

"What does your ba say about it?"

"She says, 'Just like kadu keeps you safe from diseases, a year at home keeps you free from the stares of people and the teasing of children. After a year, your widowhood will become old news, and no one pays attention to old news. It will be easy for you to face people.' But I don't agree with her. I went out all the time before I was a widow. If I were allowed, I'd walk out of the house this very minute."

"Leela, people will treat you differently because you're a widow. It can be difficult."

Maybe Ba was right. Just like Masi, others could be mean to me. It might be hard to go out. "What should I do?"

"By observing what is going around you, you can sharpen your senses. A small place gives you a chance to explore your surroundings thoroughly." She took out a notebook from her bag and gave it to me. "Tomorrow, listen to every sound you hear and write it down. It will make this year bearable."

I shook my head. "A year of keeping corner will never end. It'll be as long as a river."

"Even the river ends," she said, putting her hand on my shoulder.

I didn't know how writing down all sorts of useless sounds could help me, but Kaki had told me to be respectful. "In this notebook?" I asked.

"Yes. Also, if you know who made the sounds, and why and how, write that down, too."

I flipped the pages of the notebook; there was not one word written in it. I wondered how I'd ever have anything to write. I put the notebook in the recessed round window of the corridor.

The next day, I heard rustling in the shrubs while I brushed my teeth. A sound! I looked in its direction, but didn't see anything. After a few minutes a hen pea-cock appeared, followed by a male peacock. They hopped after each other for a while, then flew away screeching *cree ou, cree ou* loudly.

I rushed inside to write in my notebook, but didn't know what to say. Wasn't it foolish of me to write down what a pair of peacocks sounded like? Everyone had heard their screeches. What was so special about that? I closed the notebook.

I bathed and ate breakfast, then finished my math and reading. After making so many mistakes in the beginning, I was starting to do better in math. Last week I only got one problem wrong. Today I went over them carefully to make sure I did them correctly. For geogra-phy, Saviben had left a map of India for me, and I was supposed to study the rivers and mountains. I showed Ba where the River Ganga starts in the Himalayas, where

River Yamuna meets her near Allahabad, and where she becomes part of the ocean at the Bay of Bengal.

"Once you are done with your studies, Leela, could you help me churn butter?" Ba asked.

I folded the map and put it away. Ba and I stood across from each other and pulled the string tied to the long handle of the churner. The wooden churner moving in the brass pot began humming, *gham-gham*. Ba's gold bangles moved with each stroke, adding their own rhythm, *khananan khun khun, khananan khun*.

All day I tried not to think about sounds, but they were everywhere. In the kitchen, chopping, rubbing, kneading, and serving all had their own voices. After lunch, while Bapuji was asleep, I heard his snoring. The clothes hanging on a line flapped and fluttered all afternoon. All at once the bells of the temple rang out, followed by singing and music. Then the leaves whispered to the wind until I was fast asleep.

The next morning I wrote down all the sounds, just to get rid of them. I went to my corner, sat cross-legged on my rug, and began writing.

The first thing I wrote was, "The peacock is a pretty bird, but his voice doesn't match his looks." When I wrote about Ba's bangles, I looked at my arms and knew that they would never make happy sounds while churning butter. So I added, "A widow's arms are forever quiet." By the time Saviben came, I had filled a whole page with what I had heard. The last thing I wrote was, "My pencil goes *kachar-kachar* on the paper."

After we were done with the lesson, Saviben told me, "The school year is over and I am going to spend my vacation in Ahmedabad."

When I was in school, I knew summer holidays would start soon after the hot, dry wind called *loo* began to blow, but studying at home, I had not thought about it. In the house, loo was not as unbearable as it was under the open sky. The vacation had crept up silently. Saviben had been coming for several weeks now, and I had gotten used to her. Sitting in the house all day long for six weeks would get lonely. "I don't know what I'll do without your visits."

She held her hand out. "Observe and write as much as you can."

"Do I have to?" I didn't want to worry about keeping a diary. "Aren't all the sounds going to repeat every day? What's the use of writing the same thing again and again?"

"Write a sentence or two every day. You'll be surprised by how much goes on around you that you don't notice."

Then she asked if I had written anything.

I retrieved my notebook from the recessed window

and handed it to her. While she read, her fingers slid over my sentences as if she didn't want them to miss a single word.

When she came to the part, "A widow's arms are forever quiet," she stopped and took me in her arms. "I'm glad you've filled your sounds with feeling. It makes you aware of who you are. As you go on writing and expressing your thoughts, it'll open up a whole world inside of you. Your inner self is like an onion: you keep peeling it, and a new layer is always there."

It was strange to think of my inner self as an onion, and it was impossible to think of a journey I could be taking while keeping corner.

TEN

I WAS CERTAIN there wouldn't be much to write in my notebook while Saviben was in Ahmedabad. After all, a peacock's call or the sound of the churning was not going to change. I wished instead of *me* writing, that *she'd* write about the things she saw. In a big city like Ahmedabad there would be a thousand things to see, touch, and smell. There'd be hundreds of sounds to hear and new dishes to taste. But Saviben had asked me to write.

When I had tried to ignore sounds, I couldn't, and the same thing happened with scent. I began to smell things. And I continued hearing sounds, too. It was as if my ears and nose were in a race. The summer morning had its heavy, lazy smell. It was definitely different from a crisp, cool winter smell or damp, dank monsoon smell. All day long I smelled things: the wood and cow dung burning in the big *chula*; the straw on the other side of the corridor in which mangoes were nestled; burning sandalwood incense; Bapuji's and Kaka's sweaty turbans when they came home from the field; Kaki's tobacco when she stuffed it in her mouth. I wrote down all the smells. I wrote down what I saw, what I talked about, and what I heard others talk about. Slowly, I began to fill my notebook.

The scent of ripening mangoes overpowered all the other smells. When we first filled the basket with alternate layers of straw and mangoes, I turned them over every other day so the mangoes would ripen evenly, but I had to do that every day now that they were nearly ripe. That way we could eat the ripe mangoes, put the unripe ones back in the bottom of the basket, the half-ripe ones on top, and throw away the spoiled ones before they spoiled the others. It reminded me of the saying: impatience will never yield sweet mangoes.

Today, several mangoes were ripe and ready to eat. I set them aside and started putting the others back in the basket. Someone put their hands over my eyes. "Are all those mangoes for me?"

It sounded like Bapuji or Kaka, but they would never do that. "Kanubhai?" I asked.

He took his hands away and sat down beside me. "You're right. I wish you had more brothers so you wouldn't be able to tell us apart."

Kanubhai was here! It was so unexpected that I blurted, "Why didn't you write and tell me you were coming?"

"Do I have to? It's my home, too. Can't I come whenever I want?"

"If I had known a week ago I could have counted the days. There's a sweet joy in waiting."

"And what about the joy of surprise? And the argument you're having with me right now? Isn't this fun?"

He was right. This was special.

He picked up one of the ripe mangoes. "Perfect!"

"The first ones of the season," I said.

"Now every day will be a feast!"

The word *feast* sounded so strange to me. Since becoming a widow, I had not attended any dinner parties at the dharmashala celebrating marriage or janoi. I tried to imagine the coolness of cardamom on my tongue, the sharpness of cinnamon and ginger, and the scented sweetness of saffron. I couldn't. The food at home was simple. Kaki only added salt and turmeric to our vegetables and *dal*.

Ba came out of the kitchen. When Kanubhai bowed, she put her hand on his head. "It is about time you came to see how your sister was doing." Her voice was ready to crumble.

Kanubhai's smile vanished and his eyes lost their teasing sparkle. "Yes, Ba. But I'm also here to see what I can do to help her."

Kaki came, too. "May your trip be successful," she said.

Only a couple of sentences were exchanged between Kanubhai, Ba, and Kaki, but their brief conversation made me anxious and uneasy. I thought about how suddenly he had left last time after arguing with Bapuji. He hadn't visited since. I didn't want them to fight; I wanted Kanubhai to stay. That would be the biggest help of all.

Because of the heat, Bapuji and Kaka didn't come home for lunch. That day our food was plain, but a bowl of luscious slices of orange mangoes made it look like we were having a feast. "Leela," Kanubhai said, "try a piece and let us know if they are as good as they look."

I closed my eyes, took a bite, and let the flavor fill me with joy. "Even sweeter than they look."

After lunch we all rested, but I couldn't relax. I went in the kitchen to make tea. Kanubhai followed me. As I poured the water in the pot, he stared at the wall. "What are you thinking?" I asked.

Kanubhai pressed his hand on one of the pots on the top shelf and then showed it to me. "No one has used these in a long time."

There was a clear print of his palm and fingers where he had touched the pot. I gave him a towel to wipe the dust off. "You're right."

"Should we clean while we wait for the water to boil?"

"Saru," I replied

The first pan he took down from the shelf was so heavy that I had to use both my hands to carry it. It was large enough to cook dal for seventy people or more, and we didn't even have seven people in our family. I wiped it with a rag and wondered if we'd ever use it again.

"Saviben says you're improving every day," Kanubhai said.

I didn't think he had ever met Saviben and was surprised that he mentioned her. "When did you talk to her?"

He had a confused look on his face for a moment. "Kaki told me."

"Saviben makes me work hard. Harder then I did in school."

"That's good, isn't it?"

He handed me a flat brass pan. I answered as I wiped the edge. "Over the summer she wants me to write about everything that happens around our house and yard. And she said I should write how I feel."

"Are you doing it?"

"How can it help me?"

· "She's your guru. You have to respect *and* trust her."

"Like people respect and trust Gandhiji?"

"Exactly."

For a while I worked quietly, thinking about what he had said. "Do people think differently in Ahmedabad?"

He sighed. "I went to a meeting where Gandhiji talked about how men and women are equal. Everyone listened politely and nodded, but I wondered how many people actually believed it."

"How can you be sure that Gandhiji believes it?"

"One day, when I went to the ashram, he was making dough. Then he swept the kitchen."

Bapuji and Kaka never cooked, swept, or fetched water. I didn't know why a famous man like Gandhiji would do women's work unless he truly believed in equality. I wondered if any of the men who listened to Gandhiji swept the kitchen floor.

When Bapuji and Kaka came home, they were surprised to see Kanubhai. Bapuji greeted him politely but stiffly. Something was wrong. Kaka never talked a lot, so I didn't expect him to say much, but Bapuji was silent, too. After a while Bapuji, Kaka, and Kanubhai went into the drawing room and closed the door. In the past I would have peeked in the room, but not today.

I hoped they'd come out smiling after they talked, but the faces that emerged were gloomier than the faces that had gone in. Kaka said he wasn't hungry and went to bed without supper.

That evening, Ba made *fajeto*, ripe mango soup, by adding the mango pits left over from breakfast to boiling water. She added a little chickpea flour to thicken it, and flavored it with salt, ginger, and cumin sautéed in ghee. Ba filled bowls with fajeto, and Kaki served us rice and split mung beans cooked with potatoes and onion. The *clink-clank* of the serving spoons was the only sound in the room.

Our family used to be so happy when Kanubhai visited from Ahmedabad. We would all listen while he talked about what was happening in the city. I remembered when Gandhiji first decided to open his ashram in Ahmedabad, Bapuji told Kanubhai to go visit him.

For breakfast, Kaki would serve boiled milk with crunchy *charoli* nuts even though it wasn't a festival. Ba would fry plantains for the afternoon snack. After supper we would sit in the chauk and talk, laugh, and sing. All that had changed because of me. Now we had silence, and I hated it.

When I tried the soup, it didn't go down smoothly, and I had to force my throat to swallow. I wasn't going to be able to eat the rest of my supper. The kitchen was hot, and it wasn't just because of the temperature. I looked around. I saw Bapuji's scowl, Ba and Kaki's grim faces, and Kanubhai's tight jaw. How could they let their feelings burn inside their hearts instead of talking about what was wrong?

Ba tried to make me eat. "Leela, if you don't finish your food, I will give Kanubhai your share of mangoes tomorrow."

I didn't answer or even look at her. "Leela?" Kanubhai asked. He had stopped eating and was watching me.

Before I knew what I was doing, I had gotten up. "I can't eat when all of you are upset. I wish I could, I could . . . Why are you . . ." I wanted to say so much more, but my words got tangled up before they came out.

"This foolishness has to end before it makes her sick," I heard Kaki say as I ran from the kitchen.

Lakha had already made my bed, and I sat down on

my khatli. Kanubhai came in a few minutes later. "It's not your fault," he said.

"Then why are Bapuji and Kaka mad at you?"

"We disagree."

"About me?"

He sat next to me. "Yes. You know I can't stay here long, so I want you to come to Ahmedabad for a few days, but Bapuji and Kaka won't let you."

"I have to keep corner."

He looked away.

If I couldn't go with Kanubhai to Ahmedabad, I wanted him to stay with me in Jamlee. It wasn't possible, though, because if it were, he would have stayed without my asking him.

"I can't even take care of my baby sister," he said, shaking his head. "I'm useless." Tears fell from his eyes.

My brother had tried to help me. He had argued with Bapuji and Kaka on my behalf and now he had to endure their silence and disapproval. I had to be strong. "Don't worry about me," I said. "Saviben will come back soon, then I'll be busy with my studies."

"Are you sure?"

I nodded.

He was silent for a few minutes, then took a deep breath. "Leela, you can't live the rest of your life like this, and you don't have to. Think about what you want to do. There are boarding schools in Ahmedabad, and you can continue your studies there."

I was so wrapped up in keeping corner that I hadn't thought about my future. If I stayed in Jamlee, my life wouldn't change much. I'd be able to go out, but I'd always be a widow, nothing more. Kanubhai was concerned about my whole life and wanted me do something about it. I didn't know what to say. He put his hand under my chin and lifted my face. My lips trembled and I barely got the words out. "I am glad you're here now."

He brushed my tears away with his fingers.

"I want to show you something," I said to Kanubhai after our morning tea.

"Where're we going?"

I pulled his hand. "Come with me."

I took him in the back courtyard. When we were in the animal shed, I pointed to our water buffalo, Dahi.

"Now I know why you brought me here." He patted Dahi. "Looks like it won't be long before you become a mother," he told her.

Dahi made a little noise and flung her tail around. Lakha always took special care of Dahi. Not only did he feed Dahi first but he also washed and massaged her every day until her obsidian hide gleamed.

Kanubhai picked up a bunch of hay and offered it to Dahi. She chomped it down quickly.

Then Lakha came to the shed. "I heard your voices," he said.

He and Kanubhai talked about buying new wheels for the bullock cart while I fed and stroked Dahi. She felt satiny soft. As the sun beat down on the shed, the smell seemed to rise. Kanubhai and Lakha were still talking when I went in the house.

Inside the corridor, I heard Kaki say, "We can't change Leela's misfortune, but that doesn't mean we have to shatter like a broken glass. Stay home today and let's be a family again."

"You're right," I heard Kaka say.

"We'll stay home," Bapuji added.

I pretended I had not heard a word.

For lunch that day we had potatoes cooked in tamarind pulp, a salad of shredded half-ripe mangoes mixed with rock salt and black pepper, rice, mung beans cooked in buttermilk, and a bowl full of mango slices.

Everything tasted and smelled like it had before I'd become a widow.

That morning I thought about how I could make my family return to the way we used to be. I came up with the one thing Kanubhai and Bapuji agreed on. I couldn't wait to talk to Kanubhai. After lunch, when he and I were sitting alone in the drawing room, I asked, "Do you believe in satyagrah?"

"Yes. Why do you ask?" he said, picking up the newspaper from the table. He began fanning us with it.

"Bapuji has joined the Kheda satyagrah, and he says he won't pay taxes no matter what."

"I know."

"I was thinking about how you could make Bapuji not be mad at you. If you talk about satyagrah—"

He stopped fanning. "What would that do? Leela, talking about satyagrah is fine when you are sitting with other men under the kesuda tree. My fight with Bapuji is about you. I don't care if he stays mad at me for the rest of my life. He's wrong," he said, slapping the paper on the table.

I was sorry I had started this conversation. Kanubhai was so angry. "You live in a city, so maybe it's easier for you to support new ideas. It's different in Jamlee," I said.

"Maybe people here aren't ready. But I don't understand why Bapuji isn't. Doesn't he see how new ideas would help you?" Then he looked at me and said softly, "I'll make sure we all break loose from this misery."

It is tradition that a brother always looks after his sister by giving her gifts and taking care of her if she is in need. I had food, clothes, and a place to stay, so Kanubhai didn't have to do anything. In a way he was going beyond tradition. Now that I was a widow, he was also making sure I wasn't unhappy.

The next morning, Kanubhai went back to Ahmedabad, but he left something special behind for me.

Hope.

After Kanubhai left, the hot days meandered along as slowly as a pregnant buffalo. I read the newspaper to Kaka every day; the news of the war was still on the front page. Even though it was not being fought in India, we felt its effects more and more. The price of wheat, barley, fuel, and sugar had gone up, and would keep going up. Bapuji mentioned that Gandhiji had participated in the war conference and had supported a resolution on recruitment. I asked him what that meant. He explained that Gandhiji wanted us Indians to help Engrej in the war. Our other leaders, like Tilak, were opposed to this idea.

I wrote Jaya a long letter about Kanubhai's visit and told her what he had said about finishing school. At the end of the letter, I added,

I am keeping up with the news, but Gandhiji's insistence about enrolling in the British army confuses me. I agree with Tilak. Since the Engrej rule us, we have to follow their commands, but if they don't force us to fight in the war, why should we volunteer? If no one is attacking us, why should we want to kill them? And why is Gandhiji asking us to take up arms? Has he changed his mind about nonviolence?

ELEVEN

BECAUSE of the drought, we had more dry wind storms than usual. On many evenings the wind would blow and grainy dust would spin like a giant top. I wished the monsoon would come soon and calm the earth down.

Dahi was almost ready to give birth. One night I woke up, startled by what I thought were a women's screams. It was still dark, and all I could see was Ba and Kaki carrying lanterns and scurrying toward the backyard. I flung off my covers and followed them to the shed.

Lakha was sitting close to Dahi, but when Kaki or Ba got close, she kicked and tried to get up, so we all sat farther away from her. Kaki started to pray softly, and Ba and I joined her. The sound of prayer seemed to soothe Dahi. By the time she gave birth, it was nearly light out. Ba asked me if I wanted to go back to sleep.

"No, I want to pet the calf."

"You can't do that. Dahi will kick you so far, you'll end up eating dust off the ground," Ba replied.

"Let the calf nurse and I'll feed Dahi. I'll introduce you to the calf when they both relax," Lakha said. "Think of a name for her."

While taking a bath I thought of a name. When Lakha let me touch her, I whispered in her ear, "Do you like the name Mani?"

Mani seemed to like her name. She was so soft and gentle; it was hard to believe she would grow up to look like her mother.

During the day, Masi, Jivima, and many others came to see Mani. Fat Soma's wife, Pushpa, also came with Heeraben. I was used to Masi, Heeraben, or other older women seeing me, but I wanted to hide when Pushpa came. Pushpa was my age, and I didn't want her to see me in my chidri. I remembered how beautiful Pushpa had looked at the fair. Now her face was tired and colorless, as if she were sick or working too hard.

Ba offered the visitors *buri* made from Dahi's first milking after she gave birth. Ba boiled the milk, then poured it on a plate. This was the only milk that jelled. Ba cut it into pieces and offered me some, but it was springy and spongy, and I didn't want it.

Mani grew so fast that within two weeks I had

forgotten what she looked like the day she was born. I wrote about Mani in my diary so I could share it with Saviben and Kanubhai. Lakha was busy and happy, and now not only did he talk to Dahi but he also sang to Mani.

Whenever I looked at Mani I worried about what I'd seen in the newspaper. There were reports of the sarkar confiscating farmers' property and livestock if they hadn't paid their taxes. We hadn't paid ours. I didn't want the sarkar to take Dahi. If they did, Mani would lose her mother. And if Bapuji refused to cooperate, they would throw him in jail.

The monsoon finally began and the first rain soothed the earth, but we knew that it would take a lot more to soak the soil completely. All we could do was wait. One day, soon after sunrise, two men in uniform came to our house. As soon as Kaka saw them, he said to Bapuji, "Give them what they want, otherwise we will have no peace."

A shiver went through my body. I could tell they worked for the sarkar and had come to take our animals, because one of them carried a wooden staff like Lakha's. I watched them from a distance. After talking with Bapuji for a few minutes, they came in the back and told Lakha to get the bullock cart ready.

Lakha looked at Bapuji, who nodded.

Bapuji stood near the shed with his arms folded over his chest, while Ba, Kaki, and I stood by the back door. My heart raced with fear. I clutched Ba's hand.

The morning light was falling on Lakha's face, and it shone bright, but his eyes were full of the sadness of losing his best friends. Silently, Lakha hitched the two bullocks to the cart.

Without the bullocks we wouldn't be able to plow the field, and Bapuji wouldn't be able to go to the market to sell the grain. The sarkar was taking the very things we needed to farm. If we couldn't grow crops, sell them, and make money this year, we wouldn't be able pay taxes next year. It all seemed so wrong.

The man with the staff was young, but there were severe frown lines in the middle of his forehead. He pointed at Dahi and Mani and tried to lead them. They didn't move anything but their necks, which they turned to look at Lakha. The man poked Dahi in the side with his staff, but she wouldn't budge. So he hit her. Dahi let out pitiful noises. Lakha rushed to Dahi and stood between her and the man, saying, "You'll have to hit me before you hit her."

"Get out of my way," the man said, pushing Lakha to the side.

Lakha lost his balance and staggered but didn't fall. The man hit Dahi again. She raised her head. Her nostrils flared out and she fixed her gaze on the man. I was afraid she was going to attack him. Lakha put his arm on her back. Dahi lowered her head.

The man wiped perspiration from his forehead with the back of his hand. "I'll hit her again if she doesn't follow me."

Lakha's face turned as red as the morning sun, and he grabbed the man by his sleeve with one hand and snatched the man's staff with the other. "If you so much as touch her again, I'll scream until the whole town is here," he roared.

The man took a step back. "It won't stop us," he said. "We're following the sarkar's order."

"Remember, if you are cruel to animals, people will not hesitate to use force to stop you," Lakha said. His eyes blazed with anger.

The other man looked at Bapuji. "Tell your servant not to interfere in your affairs."

"He takes care of my animals, but that doesn't mean I control him. If he sees cruelty or unfairness, he has every right to protest."

"Then I'll have to file a complaint against you, because ultimately you are responsible for breaking the law," he said.

"You can do that."

"We'll throw you in jail."

"Certainly."

Lakha rubbed the buffalos' backs and asked them to go by saying, "*Khamma mari beti, chalo.*"

Dahi and Mani began walking with him as if they understood every word. Lakha led them out the back gate. When he returned, I saw him wipe his eyes.

That day we did all our chores without a word. The silence, born of sadness, was suffocating.

That night when we sat in the chauk, I asked Bapuji, "Do those men work for the sarkar?"

"Yes," he replied.

"They had no right to take our animals."

"They did. They were doing their jobs."

"They were monsters. Don't they have any mercy for the animals?"

"This is what happens when you follow orders. You have to do what you are told even if you think it's wrong."

"Where did those men take them? What if they don't feed Dahi properly? What if they separate Dahi and Mani?"

Bapuji's face turned ashen. "Don't ask such questions. They'll be fine," he replied. His voice was wobbly, as if he didn't believe his own words.

I wanted someone to ask Bapuji why he couldn't just pay the taxes and get our animals back. Ba would never say a word to him, but I thought Kaki might. I glanced at her, but she just shook her head slightly. Maybe she was certain that Bapuji wouldn't go back on his pledge. The only other person who could talk to Bapuji was Kaka, and he seemed to have given up on everything.

Kaka took out his tanpura and invited Lakha to come and sing. But Lakha stayed in his hut. This was the first time he had refused Kaka's request. There was no music that night.

I couldn't fall asleep, thinking about all the events that had led up to this. This had started when Bapuji went to Nadiad. He took a pledge in front of Gandhiji, and he was determined to keep it. I wondered if Gandhiji realized how much the insistence on truth hurt. It was difficult to fight with love when there was no sympathy. All we could do was helplessly watch those men take our bullocks, Dahi and Mani. My eyes were red and swollen in the morning.

Lakha was lost without his friends. I'd often see him sitting in front of his hut, staring into the horizon. He no longer sang. When Ba or Kaki offered him food, he'd shake his head and say, "The hunger has left me."

Kaka told him to go home to visit his family for a

few days, and one day Lakha began the two-day journey. He said he would return in a month or so.

In the third week of June, the same two men who had taken them, drove Dahi and our cart home. There was no Mani.

"The sarkar had taken so many animals that it was impossible to care for them properly. We're sorry your calf died," one of the men said simply.

And as if that were not enough, Bapuji told us, "The collector has promised that they will waive taxes for poor farmers, if the ones who can afford to pay do."

"That means we would pay," I said, handing him a cup of tea.

"Yes, I already have."

I was so disappointed and frustrated, I walked away from him.

Bapuji went to Nadiad again to mark the end of Kheda satyagrah with other farmers and Gandhiji. The newspaper reported that it was a success.

I wasn't sure how I felt about it. We lost Mani because of the Kheda satyagrah. Lakha had been humiliated, and in the end we had paid our taxes anyway. Trying to influence the sarkar had cost us too much. It would have been easier to obey the law in the first place. Maybe that's why people keep doing things the way they've always done them. It's easier to follow the old ways than to go against them.

Yet I knew that Gandhiji had brought all the farmers of Kheda together. The newspaper wrote about our drought, and the entire country knew that our crops had failed. People had never challenged the sarkar before. Maybe there was a victory in the defeat.

TWELVE

LAKHA couldn't read or write, but he managed to find someone to write us a letter that said he was getting married to a girl named Shani. He planned to return with her in a few days.

"I didn't know Lakha was engaged," I said to Ba. She was sitting on the kitchen floor peeling potatoes.

Ba pointed to a bunch of fenugreek. "Lakha has wanted to marry Shani for a long time. He must have finally talked her into it."

I sat down just outside the kitchen, where there was a slight breeze. I plucked tiny leaves of fenugreek. "How do you know?"

"I just know."

"Why did you keep it a secret?"

"It was his business, and he didn't want anyone to know," Ba replied as she sliced the potatoes.

"How could Lakha think I'm just anyone?"

"He doesn't. But you're not old enough to understand everything."

I wanted to ask Ba why sometimes I was treated
like a child and other times I was expected to behave
like a mature woman. If I was too young to be trusted
with everyday information, I was too young to be a
widow; but if I was old enough to live like a widow,
then I must be grown up.

I knew telling Ba that would only make her sad.

The sky was heavy with clouds. That night the
lightning danced, thunder rumbled, and it rained for
hours. It was the rain we'd prayed for, waited for, and
finally rejoiced over. The drought had certainly ended.
The next morning the earth was alive and her scent
rode on the wind. Oh, how I wished I could go to
our farm and get my feet muddy. I took out my notebook from the recessed window and wrote down everything, including, "I wonder if the frogs fell from the
sky, because last night I heard their croaks, *draawon,
draawon.*"

Ba went to visit Masi a few days later, and I helped
Kaki with supper. We were shelling beans when we
heard voices coming from the backyard. "Leela, see
who's here," Kaki said.

When I went to the back corridor, I saw Lakha and a young woman walking toward the house.

I ran back to Kaki. "Come quick, Lakha is home."

By the time Kaki came out, Lakha and his wife had come through the back door. The girl wore a black ghagri-poulka embroidered in bright colors and studded with round, triangular and square mirrors. Her head was covered with a black cotton odhani, the ends of which dangled down her back.

The girl's face was round with a pointed chin, and her body was bamboo-straight. She wore broad ivory bracelets of different sizes from her upper arms to her elbows and from below her elbows to her wrists. Her heavy silver anklets probably weighed more than full water pots. A *hasadi*, a wide silver necklace, rested on her collarbone, and matching round earrings covered her earlobes.

Lakha introduced her to Kaki as his wife, Shani. Then both of them bent down to touch Kaki's feet. "Be happy," she blessed them. Kaki gave me a glance before she whispered something to Shani. Even though I couldn't hear the words, I knew Kaki must have said, *"Akhand Saubhagyavati,* May you always have good luck, and may you never be a widow."

It was the blessing that every married woman expected to receive from her elders. When Lakha said to Shani,

"This is Leelaben," Shani's face broke out in a big grin, and she joined her palms in a greeting. I did the same.

"Are Dahi and Mani and the bullocks back?" Lakha asked.

"Yes, the bullocks, Dahi—"

His eyes brightened up, and before I could finish, he said, "What about Mani? Has she grown a lot?"

"Mani didn't come back," I replied, looking away. Lakha understood what I meant.

"I was afraid of that," he mumbled.

For the rest of the evening, Lakha was busy taking care of the animals. I could hear Dahi mooing in delight and the bells on the bullocks' necks ringing. Shani was inside their hut.

I sat in my corner and thought about all the jewelry Shani wore. She could only afford silver and ivory; I used to have gold.

I touched my bare fingers to my bare arms, ankles, and earlobes. That is when a lump rose in my throat. I couldn't stop the tears that followed.

The next morning, while I was brushing my teeth in the backyard, Shani stood in the doorway of her hut and called, "*Leelabon, havare vela udho sho?*"

What was she saying? Lakha and Shani were from the *Rabari* community. Traditionally, they were nomads who went from one place to another with their animals and tents. Very few of them stayed in one place like Lakha did, and they spoke Gujarati with an accent. Since Lakha had been with us for several years, his speech was more like ours, but Shani's wasn't. I repeated her words *"Leelaben, savare vehla utho cho?"* Sister Leela, do you get up this early in the morning? It took me a few seconds to say, *"Ha,* yes."

If I had to repeat everything she said to me in my head before I could answer her, then I'd never be able to talk to her, I thought. She used *H* instead of *S* and then strangely used *SH* instead of *CH*, and in some words she just swallowed the *H* completely.

She brought over a pot of milk. Now that she was here, she'd taken over milking Dahi. "Is today a churning day?" she asked Ba.

"No, tomorrow is," Ba said.

"Is there anything else you would like me to do?"

"Nothing for now."

"When you need me, please call," Shani said, and came over to where I was sitting. I glanced at her. All the ornaments she had worn yesterday were still there. A round black tattoo on her chin that I hadn't seen last night was visible in the bright morning light. Like the hazy smoke surrounding a fire, jealousy enveloped my heart, making it hard to breathe. I wanted her to leave.

And yet, she was Lakha's wife and was going to stay right here, whether I liked it or not.

"I'm going to take a bath," I said, going inside.

Shani followed me. "I'll fill up the pail with hot water for you."

I saw Shani every morning when I went in the backyard to brush my teeth. She was always there just inside or outside her hut, packing Lakha's lunch in a brass box, tying it with a piece of cloth, or whispering to him. Her anklets twinkled in the bright sunlight, her bracelets sang, and her long braid danced.

Her smile was reflected on Lakha's face.

When Lakha came home in the evening, I heard laughter and happy noises coming from their hut. Once I climbed up on a bed to clean spider webs around a window and saw Shani and Lakha eating dinner. Surrounded by the darkness, in the light of the lantern, Shani's face glowed like tamarind-polished copper, and her eyes shone like golden embers.

Lakha tried to feed Shani and she refused by covering her face. He grabbed her by the waist and pulled her close to him until she was almost in his lap. Once he had her in his arms, he stuffed the food into her mouth. I thought of how Ramanlal had fed me pooranpoli.

If Ramanlal were still alive, Ba would've taken me to the monsoon fair and countless other celebrations, and fussed over my braids and ribbons. I touched my holy tulsi bead necklace and thought of all my gold jewelry that Kaki had wrapped up in her handkerchief.

I was so engrossed in my thoughts that I didn't hear Ba calling me for dinner. Then I heard, "Leela, Leela, where are you hiding?" right behind me. I jumped down from the bed in time to see Ba standing there with a lantern in her hand. "What are you doing in the dark?"

"I'm . . . I'm . . . Nothing—"

She lifted her lantern to my face. "Your face is kesuda-red. What's the matter?"

"I . . . I don't want to be a widow," I said, covering my face.

She held her hand out and helped me climb down from the bed. "It's not in our hands to write our future."

She glanced out the window before walking me out of the room. She bit her lip. "Leela, there is nothing harder than being a young widow, but that is what you have to endure. That is your kismet. You have to be above the temptations that youth brings."

The pain of her heart had nestled in her eyes. I didn't want to make her more miserable than she already was.

I ate dinner silently.

That evening, in the stars and in the moon, in the shadows of the jamboo tree, I could see the faces of Shani and Lakha pressed together. I heard their laughter in the whispers of the wind.

When I went to bed, Shani came and asked Ba if there was any more work for her to do. I imagined savagely stripping her bangles, pulling her nose ring, yanking her necklace, and wiping her smile away.

My thoughts terrified me. I closed my eyes.

THIRTEEN

THE MONSOON had made the earth work-
able again, and it was time to plow and plant. Bapuji
and Kaka were in the field all day, and when they came
home, they were muddy, hungry, and tired. They took
baths, ate, and went to bed. Other farmers were busy,
too, and wouldn't gather under our kesuda tree to talk
and relax until the planting was done. Bapuji hoped our
peanut crop would do better than ever, and said that
maybe last year's drought was being wiped out with
this blessing from heaven.

The scent of monsoon, the *dup, dup* of water dripping from the roof, and the dance of peacocks brought
back memories. When I was little, Kanubhai would
take me to the farm after the first few rains had cooled
the earth. On the way, I'd touch the leaves of the kothimda vines that seemed to have appeared magically,

their tendrils hugging the trunks and branches of big trees.

Kanubhai would slip his arms under my shoulders, lift me up, and spin me around. The green of the plants, the yellow of the mustard blossoms, and the blue of the horizon would flow past my eyes like a kaleido-scope. On the way back from the farm, he'd pick me up, put me on his shoulders, and let me ride all the way home.

Good thing I didn't have too much time to let my mind wander, because school had started again and Saviben was back.

"I missed you," I said as soon as she walked into the house.

"I missed you too," she said, wrapping her arm around me. We walked to the drawing room.

Side by side we sat on the couch. "How was your trip?" I asked her.

"Too short. There was so much to do that I could have stayed there for months."

I was confused. "You had another job?"

"No. I volunteered with people from Gandhiji's ashram." Then she took my hand in hers. "I thought of you often, especially when I was at the ashram. If you go to Ahmedabad, you need to go there."

I nodded. "I'm glad you're back."

Saviben could only tutor me once a week now. She gave me enough homework to last until our next lesson. I wished she could come more often, but she had started teaching classes for adults and was busy with that.

The monsoon was at its peak. Sometimes I listened to the sound of the rain falling on the roof and on the chauk, mixed with the sound of peacocks calling their mates. Sometimes when the thunder rolled, it felt like a herd of water buffalo was trampling the sky. Every morning it took Ba a long time to start the fire. All the dried cow-dung patties turned soft from the humidity, and Ba had to coax the fire out of them. I shared my observations with Saviben, but after a month of monsoon, there was nothing new to discover.

Bapuji said that the Taransi River was full, and kothimda vine had sprouted everywhere. Since the backyard was soggy, I didn't go there to brush my teeth. It saved me from seeing or talking to Shani. But once I was done with my homework, with four or five days yawning in my face, my mind wandered off to her anyway. I could picture Shani singing while she cooked, she and Lakha talking softly while the rain poured outside, and her embroidering after she was done with her chores.

Sometimes I'd doodle a girl on my slate. She had

long hair and was standing under a blooming kesuda. I'd surround her with flowers and write my name under it. Sometimes I'd draw the Taransi River and the Shiva temple and people eating sweet jalebis at a fair. Other times I'd scribble a bald girl but never write my name under her. No matter what I drew, I'd wipe it off the slate before anyone saw it.

I received a short note from Jaya. I liked the part, "*I hope you've thought about what you want to study. I pray that you can go to Ahmedabad next year. It will open up a new world for you. A world where you will be Leela and nothing else.*"

Jaya had made a good point. What *did* I want to study? I could be like Saviben and help other girls. Then I wouldn't be going through life as Leela the widow— I'd be Leela the teacher. I wondered if I could do anything else besides teach. I was going to think about it.

I slipped Jaya's note in my poulka pocket and her message in my heart.

"So what have you written lately?" Saviben asked me one day.

I opened my notebook and read aloud. "At the beginning of the monsoon, the season brought and took away many things, but now, in the middle of the season, there's nothing to write. We have to hang laundry inside the house, and it takes two days for clothes to dry; the backyard smells of foul dung, and I find myself as lazy as the heavy air around me."

She raised her brows at my laziness, then relaxed them. "I like the way you're pouring your thoughts into words. It's time for you to write a poem."

I didn't know where to begin, what to say, how to say it. I did all my other homework and tried to push poetry way back in my head.

That evening, when the sun had left no light behind, I went to get a drink of water. The full moon filled the belly of the sky. Its silvery shine coated the chauk. At the chauk's edge, a red earthen pot sat on a stone ledge with a brass dipper hanging next to it. I reached for the dipper, but a soft hiss made me stop.

I listened.

There was another slow hissing sound. I looked at the dipper. Something was shining in the moonlight on top of it.

A kalotar snake!

A snake, the same kind that had killed Ramanlal, was twined around the dipper. I was paralyzed. Courage, I thought, and walked slowly backward, keeping my eyes on the snake. Then I darted to the front corridor.

"What happened?" Bapuji said. "You shake like you've seen a kalotar."

"I . . . I have. It's . . . it's . . . water dipper . . . there on the water dipper."

Bapuji was sitting with three other men, smoking bidis. They all sprang up, dropped their bidis, crushed them under their bare feet, and bolted toward the chauk. I didn't follow them. Somehow they managed to capture the snake in a jute sack. They carried it to the jungle beyond the town, farms, and pastureland and set it free. One thing we never did was kill snakes, or any other animals, for that matter.

The fear traveled from my stomach to my hands when I tried to write about it. My fingers shook so badly that my letters looked like tiny snakes.

For days after I saw the kalotar, I'd jump if I heard even a flutter of wings or the musings of the wind. I was scared of sounds. They didn't have to be loud or even real.

The fear killed my desire to write.

Heeraben came for a visit a few days after I saw the snake. The air was humid but it wasn't raining, so we sat in the chauk, eating the jamboo that Lakha had picked. The glossy purple fruit was sweet and juicy and came only in monsoon.

We were all busy eating jamboo when Heeraben spoke. She had already eaten half a dozen of them and her tongue had turned purple. She looked so funny that it was hard not to laugh. "The whole town is saying that the kalotar Leela saw was the same one that bit Ramanlal. They say the kalotar is angry with Leela and came to kill her."

My urge to laugh disappeared.

"We'll pray to Lord Rama to protect Leela," Kaki said.

"You'll need to do more than that. You must appease the snake. There is a snake pit close to the Shiva temple. You can leave some milk next to it."

"Don't you think monkeys will get to it before the snake?" Kaki asked.

"Then get a tiny snake made out of gold and offer it to a priest."

Slowly, Kaki took out her tobacco box and offered it to Heeraben. I could see that she was trying hard to control her anger. "Why should we do that?" Kaki asked as she closed the box.

"The priest will pray for Leela's safety."

"I agree that praying is the most powerful thing. We will do that ourselves."

Heeraben stood up. "I did my neighborly duty in telling you what needs to be done. Only the mother should decide how to protect her child," she said, looking meaningfully at Ba.

After Heeraben left, none of us ate a single jamboo.

That same evening, Masi rushed into the house as soon as Kaki went out. It was a windy day, and Masi's hair was frizzy. It looked like a dust storm riding on her head. She grabbed Ba's hand and took her to the drawing room. I followed them but stood behind the door. "People are whispering about the kalotar that came to kill Leela. What are you going to do?"

"I'll light a lamp and pray."

"That's what her kaki will do. Remember, you have fed Leela with your own blood. You are her mother and you must do more than chant the name of God. Besides, the town will raise a dust of talk if you don't do anything." Then she lowered her voice, and all I could hear was "wedding sari."

"Let them. I can't worry about other people or a snake," Ba said. Her voice was shaky, though. Heeraben had not been able to sway Ba, but I was afraid Masi might be more persuasive.

"When most boys are married by thirteen or fourteen, your only son is still a bachelor. Why? Because you want him to be a *pundit*! Your family has always ignored people's whispering, but you can't ignore a kalotar's hissing. You must do something to calm the kalotar, and you must do it soon, before it's too late. Do you know what I mean?"

I shivered at Masi's words. I wondered if I had done something wrong by wearing that wedding sari or thinking about going to Ahmedabad to study. I wanted to grow my hair and throw away my chidri. Maybe the snake had come to punish me for having desires that a widow should never have. I tried to think of it as a superstition, but I was still scared. My neighbors' attacks were deadlier then a kalotar's hissing.

After Masi left, Ba kept glancing at me. Her brows were tense and her eyes were dull. What was going through her mind?

Ba told Bapuji that we must perform a ceremony to appease the snake. Bapuji shook his head. "I don't believe in superstition, and I'll not succumb to it."

"Everyone says that the snake is sure to come back if we don't do it."

"Does the snake have our address and a map?"

Ba sighed deeply. "It killed Ramanlal and then it came for Leela, isn't that enough for you?"

"How do we—how does anyone know that the snake that bit Ramanlal was the same snake that came to our house? If agitated, a snake will bite. That's his nature. Our nature is to think and not get carried away with superstitions. If you want me to go with you to the temple to light a lamp and thank Lord Rama for sparing Leela's life, I'll do it. But that's as far as I'm willing to walk, and not a step farther."

That night Heeraben's words came visiting me. I told myself that Bapuji was right and I must not believe in superstition, but if Masi, Heeraben, and many others believed it, then couldn't it be true? I understood that my seeing the kalotar was just a coincidence. But the fear was stronger than reasoning. It kept me awake.

Shani was in the backyard hanging the wash when Nathu came to shave my head in the morning. I hoped she would leave. She hung a sari between me and her, creating a curtain between us. I was relieved. I didn't want her to pity me.

My head had been shaved three times since I became a widow. Today I thought about the first time Nathu had cut my hair, and how light my head had felt. Now I was used to it because my hair was never allowed to grow more than an inch. In only a few months I had completely forgotten the feel of my long, thick hair. Since Jivima had broken my glass bangles, my hands had been bare. I stared at them, realizing how much I missed the touch of cold glass against my skin.

Later, when Shani came to the house to mop the floor, I opened my books and avoided looking at her. I realized that having her around was like watching someone drink water while I was thirsty.

I took out my notebook and wrote, tears running down my face.

The death shrouds and the shadow falls,
trapping me.
I want to run
free like a newborn calf on
a grassy plain.
Tied,
I am tied with a chidri to the nail of widowhood.
Nail driven,
in the soil of my life.

Once I was done I felt better. I didn't read what I had written. And I was not going to show it to anyone. Not even Saviben.

I hoped Saviben would forget about poetry, but she didn't. After she went over my other homework, she said, "You haven't shown me one thing."

"I know," I mumbled.

She gave me a lingering look. Trying to avoid meeting her eyes, I quickly turned my face away, and my chidri slipped from my head. She tried to put it back on. I couldn't avoid her gaze. In that moment there was much said and much heard without words.

"If you don't want to write poetry, you don't have to. I understand," she said.

I ran to the corridor and brought my notebook. Before I knew it, I had flipped it open to the page where I had written the verse and handed it to her.

When she was done reading, she covered my hands with hers.

"Do I have to go on living like this forever?" I whispered.

"What would you like to do?" she asked.

I wanted to tell her about going to Ahmedabad, but an image of a kalotar came to my mind. "I don't want to live a widow's life."

"You don't have to."

I pushed the thought of the kalotar aside. "I want to study and become a teacher."

She beamed. "It is time for you to read Narmad's writing."

Narmad was a famous poet and writer who had lived fifty years ago. I doubted that his writing could make a difference in my life.

FOURTEEN

SAVIBEN brought me a book and a newsletter called *Dandiyo*. "Both of these were written by Narmad. I want you to read and think about them," she said.

I flipped through the pages of the book. "I don't know if I can finish this by next week," I said.

"There's no hurry."

After she left, I picked up *Dandiyo*. The issue had been published on September 1, 1864. There were eight pages full of Narmad's views on society at the time. On page six he'd written this about women: "If the husband is wise then the wife is considered wise, if she can produce one child, she is accomplished, if she can read the letters of the alphabet, she is educated." He went on criticizing and making fun of society's views on women. When I was done reading, I thought about it.

I reread it.

Saviben had told me that her father had been against her going to college. He said it was a man's world, and a woman's place was at home. He'd disowned her and told her he would never talk to her again. And yet she had continued school.

Kanubhai had mentioned that he'd seen the sign of the first lady doctor in the Girgam area of Mumbai. It said, "Doctor Kashibai Navrange," in big letters.

The clinic was new, and it was a great novelty. Kanubhai said many people came to Girgam just to read the board with Dr. Navrange's name on it. Some were proud to have the first woman doctor open up her practice in Mumbai, but others sighed because times were changing. Some shook their heads in shock because times had changed, and a few ignored it, believing that times would never change. How did pioneer women like Saviben and Kashibai Navrange lead the way?

Someday I could be like them, I thought to myself. A widow like me could never dream of getting married again, but I could study in Ahmedabad and become a teacher or a doctor. I had to convince my elders to let me go.

One day while sitting in the front corridor, I was so engrossed in reading the newspaper that I didn't notice Masi walking in. She stood by me, and in a mocking tone said, "Tell me what you find so exciting, Leela."

"It says here that the Kheda Farmers are busy planting their crops."

"We were blessed with ample rain so why wouldn't we? We don't need some newspaper person to tell us that. Tell me something new."

"The war is still on and—"

"The war," Masi said with a sweep of her hand, "is way over there and I don't want to hear any more about it."

I flipped the page. "Here is something about Gandhiji."

She folded her arms and gave me a cold look.

I put the paper down. "You don't want to hear about him?"

"That man is asking our people to join the British Army. He has spoken not only in Ahmedabad but in Nadiad, Karmsad, Surat. Do you think Gujarati men would pick up arms, let alone use them? How will people who eat dal and rice because they don't want to slaughter animals be able to kill human beings? Their parents will never give them permission to fight. It is a bad idea. If you ask me, Gandhiji is wasting his time."

Masi's response knocked all the sense out of me. Not only was she the last person I'd have expected to know the latest news, but her own opinion of the situation surprised me. I agreed with her completely. That was a strange feeling for me. "You're right," I managed to say.

"Of course I am. The men with radical ideas think they can change the world in an instant. That Narmad was one of them. Now there's Gandhiji."

Was it just a coincidence that I was reading Narmad, and Masi mentioned him?

"I just hope your brother doesn't decide to join the army," Masi said.

My heart skipped a beat. "Kanubhai?"

"He's in Ahmedabad and is influenced by Gandhiji a lot more than we are. And he has that strong will from your father's side of the family. I wouldn't be surprised if he showed up in an army uniform, asking for permission to fight in the war."

Stop it, I screamed inside. To Masi I said, "So you think he would ask for permission before he joined the army?"

"I suppose," she said, tucking her hair behind her ear.

I was done talking to Masi. She stood there for a minute, but I picked up the paper again. She walked toward the kitchen, looking for Ba.

* * *

The rains were tapering off. The dawn was dressed in pink-gold and the dusk in purple-silver. With the breeze swaying the thousands of leaves of the jamboo and kesuda trees, even the afternoons were comfortable. Shani decorated the outside mud walls of her hut with paintings. She used shades of kesuda and mustard blossoms, peacock's feather and kothimda vines. Every day I saw new pictures.

One afternoon I watched Shani paint the wall while everyone rested. She turned to me and, sweeping her ivory-covered arms, said, "Leelabon, why do you watch me from so far away? Come, come close to me."

"I can see all I want to see from here," I replied. Still, I was curious about her paintings. How did Shani mix colors? Who had taught her to draw like that? How did she decide what to paint?

She walked toward me. "It's true that a mountain looks lovely from a distance."

She pulled at my hand, bare as the branches in autumn.

"From here you can't see all the parrots and sparrows I've drawn. You don't see the feet of the goddess Lakshmi or the eye of the peacock's feather. You miss the details."

I let her drag me.

As we stood in front of her paintings she talked about each one and what it meant. She was right: I'd observed little from a distance and understood even less. As she told me about the art, her gaze brightened as if the colors had flown from the walls and nestled in her eyes.

When I turned back, she put her arms around my waist. Her fingers touched my bare back. I pulled away as if they were burning coal.

"Your body is unhappy?" she asked.

"Let me be," I said, ripping her hands from my waist. I ran through the chauk, passing the corridor, and dove onto my bed. The darkness of the room and the tears streaming down my face found comfort in each other's company.

I fell asleep on the bed and dreamed I was going to Ramanlal's house for the first time, dressed in a new sari. It was the bright red of the sun peeking out from the horizon, of freshly crushed cayenne peppers, of Ba's ruby earrings. And the white was the white of sunshine, of jasmine blooms, of Kaki's diamond nose ring. Ramanlal was dressed in golden silk, like he had been that night in the dharmashala.

Before we entered his house, his mother came outside to welcome us as a couple. She carried a small platter containing vermilion powder, uncooked rice, and a flickering lamp. Dipping her ring finger in vermilion, she made a dot on his forehead and then on mine. Then she took the rice and stuck it on top of the vermilion for good luck. A few rice grains fell and landed on Ramanlal's nose, dotting it red. I covered my face with my sari and suppressed a giggle. As we stepped over the threshold, I stumbled, and Ramanlal caught me before I fell down.

After running away from Shani, I talked to her only when I had to. It wasn't easy to do, because, without my asking, Shani brought hot water for my bath and helped me grind millet. When I struggled to fold saris and turbans, she held the opposite ends so they didn't drag on the floor. She was nice and I was cold. I knew that, and still I kept my silence.

I could forget about Shani when I was surrounded by people. She was there and yet not there, but when I was alone, her presence loomed like the sun. There was no relief from her.

I burned in her radiance.

One day, Kaki and I were applying castor oil to rice so it wouldn't spoil. "You don't like Shani, do you?" she said.

Kaki's question dropped on my lap so suddenly that it took me a moment to answer. "I don't like the racket

Shani makes when she walks," I said, rubbing the pile of grains with my oily hands.

"She talks too much?"

I moved my sticky hands through the pile of rice. "No."

"Then what?"

"She's just noisy. All the things she wears give me a headache."

Kaki began filling the iron barrel with the oily rice, but she looked at me as if she were measuring my insides.

"Do you think she's bothered by your being born into a brahman family?"

I picked up a brass pan and scooped up rice. "Would she be? I never thought of that."

"Remember that Shani is Shani and you're you," she said.

"It is not just that. She's always happy, and it makes me miserable."

"So you try to make her unhappy by being rude?"

I looked away. "I guess."

"You must be stronger than that."

As I filled up the pail with rice and emptied it in the barrels, I thought about what Kaki said to me. I was being unfair to Shani.

Lakha told us that Shani was with child. There was a

brightness in his eyes, as if he were already holding his baby. Shani's face shone with a dreamy light, and her stone-hard, palm-flat belly had taken on a soft curve. I envied her more than ever. Even though I had been a wife once, I would never be a mother.

I had promised myself to be kind to Shani, and I greeted her with enthusiasm in the morning. She broke out in a grin like the day she met me. It made me feel good. Later, I helped her with the milking, talked to her about Dahi and the bullocks, and helped her with folding turbans and saris. It was not enough, but I had begun.

One afternoon I started reading the book by Narmad that Saviben had given me. I'd studied some of his poems and read his *Dandiyo* newsletter, but this was an entire book, and I could read only a little at a time. Narmad's ideas were strong and strange and must have gathered in his heart the way clouds gather in the sky.

He said that childhood marriage was a shameful thing and should be abolished right away. He believed that widows should be allowed to marry again. He must have been a smart and courageous man to think of things like that and then write them down.

As his ideas sank into my mind like monsoon rain into soil, thoughts began to grow. It was not right that I had to give up everything, including my own hair. If there were other people who thought like Narmad did, and were not afraid of society, then there was hope for me.

Narsi Mehta's *bhajan*, devotional song, that Kaka loved, said we were all part of the same god. If it was true, then widowed men and widowed women should be treated the same. Maybe some traditions started as silk threads but had turned into stubborn ropes. If I was questioning them, then others could be, too.

I was afraid that these rapidly growing thoughts would cover every inch of my mind. Narmad's ideas were so radical that many people would oppose them. I was just a powerless young widow, and people would shun me if they found out that I agreed with Narmad.

I closed the book and went into the backyard. Right outside her hut, Shani sat embroidering, with her feet stretched out in front of her and a pillow propped behind her back.

"Leelabon, come," she said when she saw me.

"Do you want some tea?" I asked as I walked toward her.

"*Ho've*, sure," she sang out.

"Then let's go in the house."

I picked up her pillow and embroidery, and she brought her teacup along. Shani sat just outside the kitchen while I made tea.

"Leelabon, what do you read all day long?"

I got the book and held it out to her. She shook her head. "We don't learn to read and write."

"Lakha had told us that. I forgot."

"Do you like reading?"

"I do. I can become a teacher or doctor only if I study."

"A teacher? Like Savibon?"

"Yes."

Shani was quiet for a while.

I wondered if Shani thought that was impossible—or shameful.

The tea was done. She held her cup out to me, and I poured the tea. I took mine in a German-silver cup and sat next to her.

She blew on her tea and took a small sip. "Good tea." She flipped pages of the book with her left hand. "Is this the story about Lord Rama and Sita?"

"No."

"Then what's it about? Even though we don't read, our elders tell us stories about Lord Rama and Sita and about the fight between Rama and Ravana. We learn about Lord Krishna and how he stole butter, and how he destroyed the evil king Kansa. We listened to so many stories that if you wrote them in the sky, they'd fill it up and there'd be no room left for the stars."

"There are other stories besides the ones you know."

"Then tell me a story from this book."

"This book doesn't have any stories. It's just writing."

"If it's not a story, what's there to tell?"

So I explained to Shani what I'd read that afternoon. "It says here that, like men, women should have rights to education; and like widowed men, widowed women should be allowed to marry again."

"*Chee, chee,*" she said. "How can people of high caste like you even think about it? If you married again, then you'd be like us."

I almost dropped my teacup. "Do Rabari widows get remarried?"

"Yes. I was married at three. My parents gave me my anu when I was fourteen. My husband was always sick, and even though we lived together for three years, he was too weak to give me any children. After he died, Lakha asked for my hand, and my bapuji wanted me to marry him, but I said no for two years. Once you've tied a knot with one man and gone around the sacred fire, it takes a while before you want to take another man."

"But you're married now."

"When Lakha came last summer, he asked again. He'd waited a long time. It meant he had real feelings for me, and so I said yes."

"Did you have feelings for him?" I asked.

"Yes," she whispered. "They were slow to come, but now he is everything to me."

I couldn't believe that Shani was a widow like me. She had not been born into a brahman family and that was why she could marry again. If I were Shani's sister, I wouldn't be wearing a chidri and have a bald head. What good was it to belong to the highest caste if you had to suffer?

The next thing I knew, Shani was saying, "Leelabon, Leelabon?"

"What?"

"I was afraid you were lost."

"Lost where?"

"In your thoughts. Our elders say that when that happens to someone, you have to bring them back. Tell me what you were thinking."

"I was thinking how you had a second chance to marry, but I'll always be a widow. It makes me sad."

"I'm sad for you, too," she said, and held my hand.

"If you can remarry, why can't I? If brahman men can remarry, why can't brahman women? Why can't women be treated equally to men?"

"How can they? Men are fire and women are water."

"Fire and water are equally dangerous, but without them we can't survive. And what stops fire? Water."

She listened, and with my every word, her eyes dilated until they were as wide as lemon slices.

"Does this book tell you all these things?"

"No, but it tells me one thing, and then my own thoughts lead me to a second thing and then on to a third thing. When you read books like these, they make you think."

"I can't read. I can only embroider. That's what I've been taught."

"But you do such beautiful work. Besides, the other day you told me some of the designs were yours."

"Yes," she said, her eyes sparkling like the pieces of mirrors, *abhla*, she had stitched on a piece of cloth.

"I wish I could embroider abhla and draw like you."

"I'll teach you, and if you want—"

"I'll teach you how to read and write," I said.

We started our lessons right away.

In the beginning, when I tried to stitch on an abhla, it slipped out and fell off. Shani giggled as I searched for the missing piece. "Shani, laugh all you want now, but someday I'll get as good as you. I'll stitch them by the hundreds."

"Ho've," she said. "But let me laugh now while I can. Your turn will come when you teach me to read all those rows of black on white paper."

"I won't laugh." I started over on the abhla with a yellow thread as bright as a mustard blossom.

I wove my thread in and out around the tiny piece of mirror. The stitches weren't even, like Shani's, but the abhla stayed in place. "Why do you call a piece of mirror an abhla?" I asked, picking up another one.

"Abhla comes from *abh*, the sky," she said, pointing up. "At night our whole *nesdo*, camp, gathers under the sky. The earth is our mother and the sky is our father. We try to bring pieces of the night sky to earth."

"Is that why you use black for the background color?"

"Yes."

I thought of how Saviben's eggplant-purple sari with gold, the one I called nisha-akash sari, reminded me of the sky, and how the sparkle of abhla reminded Shani of the night sky. I realized that night sky filled us both, Shani and me, with the same wonder.

When I taught Shani how to read the letters one at a time, *ka, kha, ga, gha* . . . she'd mix them up, and instead of reading her name *Shani* she'd read it *Khagi*, and instead of reading my name *Leela*, she'd read it *Beeba*, and we'd both laugh until tears gushed out of our eyes.

Slowly, though, she got better, and when she read, her face lost the puzzled look, and she didn't squint and stutter. "My baby's going to be smart," Shani said.

"How do you know?"

"Because I'm learning to read, and my baby is listening in there. Arjun's son, Abhimanyu, was a great warrior because he heard the battle plan from Lord Krishna while he was still in his mother's womb."

Shani could read only a sentence or two, but her face was beaming with the conviction that her baby was going to be brilliant.

At supper, Kaki said, "Shani has found a guru."

"Who is it?" Bapuji asked.

"Leela?" Kaka said.

"I'm not a guru. I'm teaching her the letters."

"Shani is smart. If she were a brahman girl, she would be reciting Sanskrit verses," Kaki said.

I wanted to say, *But then she would be a widow like me.* Instead I said, "Yes."

"Unlike money, knowledge increases many folds when you part with it," Kaka said.

Ba's eyes glowed. "Shani is your first student, Leela."

"And I am Shani's. She's teaching me mirror-work."

Kaki squeezed my hand. "You've made me so proud," she said.

One day when Shani was showing me her homework, Lakha came into the chauk. "If my wife studies as much as you do, she will rule over me," he said to me.

"If you didn't want her to learn, why did you buy her a new slate?" I asked.

"How could I refuse her? It is the only thing she has ever asked me for."

"Shani is learning fast, so you'd better start listening to her now."

Lakha's face glowed as he looked at Shani.

Shani laughed and told Lakha, "You've got nothing to worry about. It will take me two lifetimes to learn as much as Leelabon."

"Then I have some time," he said as he walked away.

From the newspaper, I had learned that Gandhiji's efforts to enlist young men in the army had failed. Masi was right about Gujaratis not wanting to send their sons to fight the war for the Engrej, especially those from Kheda, who had not forgotten how badly the sarkar had treated them during the drought. Many were angry at Gandhiji for abandoning his message of nonviolence.

But Gandhiji was steadfast in his determination. He believed that as loyal subjects of the British Empire, we had to cooperate. He traveled around Gujarat with a man named Patel to enlist young men in the army. No one supported them, and they had to walk many miles, eat meager food, and sleep on the floor. This made

Gandhiji gravely ill, and he was rushed to Ahmedabad.

We received a letter from Kanubhai. He mentioned that, like many other people, he had tried to visit Gandhiji but couldn't. Gandhiji was very weak and was allowed to see only a handful of people. The mood in Ahmedabad was grim.

Kanubhai also wrote that he would be coming home soon. He had not mentioned joining the army. Masi was wrong about that.

FIFTEEN

"LESS THAN six months left to keep corner," I wrote in my notebook. I flipped back to read what I had written before. My own words brought the past summer and monsoon alive. How did I feel so connected to the world when I couldn't go beyond our house and the backyard? Unlike the widowhood that had thrown me into instant despair, this change had come slowly, like music building, gradually, softly.

It was the month of *Asso*, and Diwali was fast approaching. Diwali was our biggest holiday, celebrating Lord Rama's return after fourteen years of exile.

On the eleventh day after the full moon, I was folding the laundry in the chauk when I heard the gate open. Ba and Kaki were in the kitchen, and Bapuji and Kaka had already gone to the farm, so I thought Masi had come for a visit.

It was Kanubhai.

I rushed toward him with a half-folded turban in my hands. "What's in there?" I said, pointing to a brass container he was carrying.

"All you care about is what's in here? How about asking how I am?" he said as he stretched his free arm and wrapped it around my shoulder.

"You look healthy to me," I said, looking up at him.

He laughed and exchanged the turban for the container. "Open it."

The container was heavy so I set it down. I kneeled in front of it. As soon as I lifted the cover, the scent of saffron filled the air. I peeked inside. It was full of round *pendas*, my favorite sweets. We didn't get pendas in Jamlee. It was made by boiling milk until it thickened and turned into a solid, then adding sugar and spices to it. The yellow rounds were dotted with dark cardamom seeds, and the center of each one was studded with blanched half-almonds. I took one out, broke it in two pieces, and put one half in Kanubhai's mouth and one in mine.

The moist, grainy cardamom flavor burst in my mouth, then the subtle taste of saffron melted sweetly.

"You're the best brother."

He finished folding the turban. "If you are trying to flatter me so you can have another penda, it won't work."

"If you didn't want me to have them, who did you bring them for?"

He put the turban on the side. "Of course, I brought them for you. And also to share with people when they visit us."

It was nice that the two of us had a few minutes together, and I didn't want to ruin it by reminding him that no one would visit us for Diwali this year.

Kaki didn't say a word when she saw all the pendas, but Ba did. "I don't know why you bought so many. Have you forgotten that we're still in mourning, and Leela is keeping corner? We're not supposed to celebrate Diwali."

"Ba, I'm here to enjoy the holidays with Leela, and I will. Besides, men gather under our kesuda tree every night, and Heeraben, Masi, and Jivima come to our house often, don't they? It's ridiculous that they won't visit on Diwali because—"

Ba didn't let him finish. "That's how it is here."

"And if we don't do anything, it will always stay that way. The whole world will change except for Jamlee."

"This is not your Ahmedabad, and Gandhiji doesn't live here." Ba's raised eyebrows and her stern expression were harsher then her words.

I stared at the floor. It was painful to listen to Ba and Kanubhai argue.

He started to say something to her, then changed his mind. He lifted my chin and said, "Leela, I am sorry. I hate to do this to you, but if no one calls on us, the two of us will have to finish the pendas."

Then he took out another one and fed us both half.

That night Kaka played tanpura and I played *manjira*, finger cymbals, while Kanubhai sang "Bhajan," written by the poet Narsi Mehta. Lakha and Shani also joined us.

"*Akhil Bramandma, ek tu shrihari*
Jujve roop anant bhase."
In this whole universe you are the only god
Yet, you manifest in infinite varieties and forms.

The tinkling of the manjira was set off by Kanubhai's rich voice like stars over the deep purple sky, illuminating it just so. Then Kaka asked me to sing. At first my voice wavered, but it slowly gained strength. When I was done, no one said a word for a few minutes. Then Ba reached out and touched my hand. Bapuji cleared his throat. "That was beautiful, Leela."

I was happy. I cherished the rare compliment Bapuji gave.

When I went to bed and closed my eyes, the sound

of my family's music was gone, but the magic still hung in the air.

Last Diwali, Kanubhai and I had gone to the market and bought ground gypsum dyed in rainbow colors. It felt like fine-grained salt. We made a *rangoli*, a colorful geometric design out of the powders, and laid it out on the ground in front of the house. I had filled the big triangles with purple, and the squares with ocean blue, and outlined the entire design with ruby red. We had wrapped up the extra colors in old newspaper and saved them.

Because I was keeping corner, I wasn't supposed to enjoy festivals or make a rangoli, but the day before Diwali, Kaki took out the leftover colors and told me and Kanubhai to use them up.

"What would people say?" I asked.

"If you make a rangoli in a corner, no one will see it."

"I think that is an excellent idea," Kanubhai said. His brown eyes shone with a mischief I hadn't seen for a long time.

So I swept one corner of the chauk clean, while he opened up all the packages. "Let's draw trees, flowers, and a river," I said to him.

"And a dancing peacock," he added.

We began working in the late afternoon when the

sun was on the other side of the house behind the jamboo tree.

"It's amazing how much time we're spending on a design that will only last a few days," I said, filling in roses with red gypsum powder.

"When you were little, it took you ten minutes to fold a sheet. You would make sure the ends matched perfectly and that there were no creases. I used to tell you it didn't matter, because the next day we were going to have to unfold it anyway. But you wouldn't listen."

"I wanted to do a good job."

"What about now? Don't you want to make a beautiful rangoli?" he asked, touching my cheeks with his fingers. Then he laughed. "Your cheek looks like a jamboo."

I touched my face.

"Now it is purple and red mixed together," he said.

Only my brother could make me wear red and purple again!

"I've been thinking. I *would* like to go to boarding school in Ahmedabad. Do you think Bapuji and Kaka would let me?" I asked Kanubhai.

"You worry about doing well in the exams and leave the rest to me," he said.

"What will you do if Bapuji and Kaka say no?"

"I'm not worried about Kaka," he replied. He stopped coloring and straightened up. His jaw tightened as he gazed far away. "And Bapuji *has* to say yes."

I watched Kanubhai take a pinch of brown. As he moved his hand up and down between the lines, filling it with the powder, a tree trunk came alive. Someone could step on it by mistake the next day and mess it up, but at that moment, it was perfect.

The day after Diwali, on New Year's Day, Kaki insisted we sit in the parlor. "All our lives we've used the drawing room for visitors; starting today, we will use it for ourselves," she said.

"You mean every day?" I asked.

"It's part of our house just like the kitchen and bedrooms, isn't it? Yes, we'll always keep it open."

I straightened the sheets and plumped the pillows on the couch. It felt strange to think that the room was for us now.

We didn't expect any guests, but Saviben and Fat Soma came to wish us *"Saal Mubarak,* Happy New Year." Saviben was first. When she arrived, everyone had already gone to temple except for me and Ba. My heart missed a beat when I saw Saviben in a white sari like the ones Gandhiji's followers wore. Without even touching it, I could see that it was thick and rough. "How do you like my New Year's resolution?" she asked me, her face sparkling.

"You mean the hand-spun cotton sari?" I asked.

"Yes. This summer when I was in Ahmedabad I wore only *khadi* saris. After coming back, I started wearing my other ones again, but they didn't feel right."

Saviben had definitely been influenced by Gandhiji, but why did she have to give up the colors we both loved? I could tell she was proud and happy about her decision, though. "You look nice in white," I told her.

Ba served tea. "Will you go to the ashram in summer?" she asked Saviben as we drank.

"Yes."

"It is hard for me to believe that people of different castes cook and eat together in the ashram."

"That's what makes it feel like a family. Everyone is a human being there."

Ba shook her head. She didn't approve of us eating food cooked and served by lower castes, but she didn't say anything.

Saviben took out a package from her bag. She handed it to me, saying, "I'm sorry to bring you this. I wish I could . . . I could have brought you something else."

"Why? I'd like anything you brought me," I said, untying the cloth.

A silk chidri slid out and tumbled onto the floor, its folds opening up like a fan. Unlike a cotton chidri, the brownish-red silk shimmered and twinkled. Since becoming a widow, this was the most beautiful cloth I'd received. I gathered it up to my cheek. It was soft, softer than powdered vermilion.

I showed Saviben the rangoli Kanubhai and I had made.

"I'm glad your brother came. There are some memories you will never part with. For you, celebrating this Diwali with your brother will be one of them," she said.

"I'll never forget the day you came to talk to Ba and Kaki, and offered to teach me. I didn't really want to study then, but now I know it was the best thing that ever happened to me," I said.

She pulled me close. I didn't mind her rough khadi palav rubbing against my cheeks.

Masi came in while Saviben was leaving. I watched them talk just inside the wooden gate for a few minutes. I couldn't hear what they said, but I assumed they wished each other "Saal Mubarak."

Masi didn't mention Saviben, and that was good. On New Year's Day we were supposed to overlook our differences and embrace each other with open hearts. Maybe that was what Masi was doing.

When Fat Soma came, he bowed to Kaka, Kaki, Bapu, and Ba. Kaki gave him a silver rupee, and I offered him a penda. He took one and sat down on the couch.

Then he took out a handkerchief and placed the penda on it.

"Has Pushpa gone to her parents' house?" Ba asked him.

"No, she isn't feeling well, otherwise she would have come with me."

As we talked, I noticed that Fat Soma played with the fringe of the pillow with one hand.

"Aren't you going to eat?" I asked, pointing at his other hand, which held the handkerchief.

He looked at it and hesitated for a second, then mumbled, "You don't get such good penda in Jamlee. I'm going to share this one with Pushpa."

Kanubhai winked at him. "If you eat one, I'll give you two to bring Pushpa."

His crooked tooth poked out as he smiled. "What if I eat two?"

"Then you can have four for her."

Ba put several pendas in a *padio* and gave Fat Soma a package, saying, "Pushpa and you can enjoy these together, but don't tell anyone else who gave them to you, okay?"

"I understand."

Before Fat Soma left, he said to me, "I'm glad I came."

"Me too."

Even though Fat Soma was embarrassed to show it, his love for Pushpa shone through. He was worried about her. I was surprised that I wasn't jealous of them. I wanted them to be happy. Not because I had learned to accept my fate, but because I wasn't bitter anymore.

Kanubhai left two days later. That afternoon I wrote in my notebook, "The Diwali I wasn't supposed to celebrate is over. This year I have truly understood the meaning of it. The whole world seems brighter."

SIXTEEN

A WEEK after Diwali, I was sitting in the chauk reading, when Masi stopped by. "I saw your kaki walking to the temple, and thought I'd visit my sister for a few minutes."

I pointed to the kitchen. "Ba is in there."

She didn't move. "What are you reading, Leela?"

I handed her the issue of *Dandiyo*. She looked at it for a few seconds before giving it back to me. "Who gave you this?"

Masi's and Narmad's ideas were far apart. She had called him radical. But I acted as if I didn't know that. "Why, do you like Narmad's writing? I have a book I can give you."

Masi's face became tense.

Ba came out of the kitchen wiping her hand on a

piece of old sari. "I thought I heard your voice," she said to Masi.

Masi turned to Ba. "Did you know your daughter is reading Narmad?"

"What about it?"

"I will tell you what! Some people call him a writer and a poet, but he's nothing but a firebrand. The schools spread his radical, shameful ideas faster than gossip under a banyan tree."

"Masi, I don't think—"

Masi cut me off and said to Ba, "Sister, you don't want what happened to Kaveri from Balasinor to happen to Leela, do you?"

Kaveri was a widow like me. Two years ago, when she was fourteen, she ran away with a barber and was now living with him in the town of Disa, far away from her family. There were rumors that he treated her badly.

Masi continued, "A brahman widow running away with a lower-caste boy. Such a stain! Not only for her family, but for the whole caste. Who knows what she is suffering now? And you know why it happened, sister? It happened because Kaveri was given too much freedom. After her year of keeping corner, she went back to school and passed the barbershop every day. It probably started with nothing but eye contact, a hand gesture, mouthing a word or two, but it led to disaster."

"What does Kaveri running away have to do with Leela?" Ba asked.

"Everything! If Leela is fed such bold ideas, then she is sure to become unmanageable."

"Leela still has four more months to keep corner. And even when she goes out, she won't do anything to shame us," Ba said.

"Do you think Kaveri's ba thought that Kaveri would? And sometimes the girls are not to blame. There are men who force themselves on a woman, especially on a young widow. No one thinks it could happen to them, yet it does. How many girls get pregnant and end up jumping into a well and killing themselves? How many are silently killed by their own family when they find out that she has disgraced them? Too many! There's always a man behind their predicament whom we never see."

Ba's face turned glum.

Masi lowered her voice. "You have enough to provide Leela for seven lives. I know you've all been taken in by Saviben. I'd never allow such a modern woman in my house. On the New Year, instead of wearing a red or purple silk sari with gold work, why did she wear a white khadi?"

"She is a follower of Gandhiji," I replied.

Masi gave me a stern look. "Don't interrupt me, Leela. Don't you see Saviben is smitten by politics? I ask, is this a woman's concern? If she was supposed to fight for our rights, the Lord would've made her a man."

"Kanubhai says that in the city, men and women are both taking part in politics. It's just a matter of time before it comes to towns like ours," Ba said.

"Your Kanubhai is another one with modern ideas. Does he realize we can't win a fight with the Engrej? Tell me, did we gain anything from the Kheda satyagrah? The British are smart people. They have to be, to rule us from five thousand miles away. Have any of our people gone that far and ruled them? If our men want to battle for more rights, so be it, but we women better stay at home and make meals."

"You know the queen of Jhansi, Rani Lakshmibai, fought the British," Ba said.

"And what happened to her? Some people say she died fighting for her country and became *shaheed*. Maybe a queen like her can become a martyr, but Saviben is no queen. And she has no right to feed her beliefs to her young students, spreading her ideas through their minds like poison."

"You're exaggerating. I think—"

"I'm not. Believe me, that's how it is. I consider

Leela to be like my own, and it gives the pit of my belly a pain to imagine what could happen to her someday. Take my advice or leave it, it's up to you. It's my duty to tell you, and after this my mouth is stitched shut. But I do feel better banging my head open and spilling my thoughts."

Ba didn't reply.

"Think about it," Masi said. "Don't forget the pigs of gossip. If you feed them, you'll have to chase them."

I finally retorted. "What gossip? I haven't stepped out of the house for months. If people still want to talk about us, let them. We can take care of ourselves. You don't need to meddle in our affairs."

"Leela, don't talk to your masi like that," Ba said. Her voice was sharp as a knife. Then she turned to Masi and added, "Enough! Let us live in peace."

Masi opened and closed her mouth twice, but no words came out. Before leaving, Masi warned Ba, "You . . . you've spoiled Leela. You must never spoil a widow. You know what they say: 'An indulged brahman widow is lost to her family.' Is that what you want?" Then she marched out without waiting for a reply.

After Masi left, silence fell between Ba and me. I was furious. Why was Masi telling Ba that I shouldn't be influenced by Narmad and Saviben's radical ideas when she was pouring her own old-fashioned ideas into Ba's head?

Ba glanced at the kitchen. "I'll make supper."

Usually I helped Ba, but today I didn't.

SEVENTEEN

SAVIBEN had made me read the newspaper for homework for many months, and now I was addicted to it. I learned that this year the Kheda farmers were going to have a good harvest. Gandhiji was still sick but was out of danger. In November the war ended and they didn't need more soldiers.

When I first started reading the news, it made no difference to me how the farmers were doing, what our leaders did, or who won or lost the war. Now I understood that events were like the spokes of wheels. Even if a single spoke did not seem critical, it was still part of the wheel that moved the world from the present to the future.

I was affected by last year's drought—Bapuji's joining Gandhiji's satyagrah, Mani's death, the abundant rain this year, the war and rising prices because of it: all were tied to my life. The ample crops and peace would be good for everyone, I hoped.

I received a letter from Jaya.

Dear Leela,

You haven't written to me in a long time. How are your studies going? Will you be ready to take the exams? Kanubhai paid us a surprise visit last week. He gave us all the news in detail. I hope you'll be in Ahmedabad in a few months. Then I can see you, because we live only two hours from the city.

Are you reading the newspaper? I am. I feel that even though we can't meet, now we're connected by everything that's happening to our country, our world.

Write to me and let me know how you are.

With love,
Jaya

Jaya was excited about my going to Ahmedabad and being able to see me often. The thought made me happy, but I still didn't have permission to go. If Bapuji refused, nothing else would matter.

I wrote Jaya a reply and told her I was studying hard for my exams. I ended the letter telling her I couldn't wait to see her this summer.

I hoped our desire to see each other was so strong that it would make the meeting happen.

This year the cold arrived late, but when it came it swished through every corner of the house with crisp, chill air. It seeped into the floor and stretched out on the beds. It settled on brass plates and hid in my chidri. Ba gave me two thick chidris and wool poulkas with long sleeves to keep me warm.

Lakha lit the fire in the backyard every morning, and Shani fed it with brush and dried cowdung patties, until midmorning when the sun warmed up the day. When I sat by the fire to brush my teeth, she greeted me with "Jai Shri Krishna," and we both huddled close to the fire to stay warm.

Shani and I spent afternoons together in the chauk. She'd sit with two or three pillows propped behind her back and do her homework while I embroidered. That way we were there to help each other. Shani could read and write simple sentences now, and was learning numbers and addition, while my abhla pieces looked perfect and were surrounded by even stitches.

Some days Shani would declare a holiday from studying and make stuffed toys for her baby. She would take a piece of brightly colored fabric, fold it in two, then draw a bird or an animal on it. She would cut out the shape and sew the two parts together, leaving a small opening. Then she would stuff it with cotton. She could make two or three of them in one afternoon. Sometimes she would appliqué a red beak on a parrot or stitch abhla on the back and sides of an elephant.

Then I'd make tea, and we'd talk while drinking it.

I'd always make tea and pour it in the cup that Shani brought with her. It felt strange to think that if we both lived in the ashram, I could drink the tea that Shani made, and we would share our utensils. If there were no difference between us in the ashram, then I would be able to marry again, just like Shani had.

Lakha took Shani to her parents' house in the beginning of January. He would come back right away, but she would spend the last few weeks of her pregnancy there and return after the baby was at least a month old. I gave Shani a hug and said, "Come back soon."

"I'll come back as soon as my mother says I can travel."

Without Shani, there was no rhythm to my days.

EIGHTEEN

AFTER SHANI left, I took over some of the chores that she did. In the morning I helped Ba with churning and Kaki with grinding millet and wheat. I also swept and mopped the floor. Even with the extra work, the days were dull. I was glad when Kanubhai came for a visit in the middle of January. This was the first time he had returned since Diwali. I could tell that something was on his mind, because he couldn't sit still long enough to talk to me or look me in the eyes.

We ate thin crepes made of wheat flour and spicy ones made of chickpea flour. "Will you stay all week?" I asked.

"I have to go back in two days."

"Will you come home this summer?"

"I don't know. How about if you come to Ahmedabad?" he asked.

"Me?" I clapped my hands and smiled. I remembered Jaya's letter. When Kanubhai visited her, he must have told her that he was going to take me to Ahmedabad. "It would be wonderful to spend the summer with you, and I can see Jaya, too."

Ba stopped spreading the batter on the skillet. "Don't make Leela promises about the summer that you can't keep."

"Why wouldn't I keep it? I'll come back to take her."

"Remember, you have not asked your bapuji or kaka yet," Ba said.

The muscles of his jaw became tense, and his eyes filled with anger. After that the steam from the skillet made soft hissing noises while we ate in silence.

Kanubhai had always treated Ba with tender respect. It seemed to have disappeared. Even though he didn't argue with her, I could tell he was furious. He ate very little and drank three tumblers of water. It was as if he were trying to douse the anger that burned within him.

In the afternoon, Kanubhai, Bapuji, and Kaka stood under the kesuda tree. From inside the house, I watched their faces leaning toward one another, their lips fluttering, their feet firmly planted on the ground. Sometimes Kanubhai moved his hands like a warrior's sword, at other times he ran his fingers down the bark of the tree and a couple of times he covered his face with his hands. They stayed out there for two hours.

Later, Kanubhai whispered to Ba and Kaki in the drawing room.

I wanted to ask Kanubhai what they had said, but I never got the chance, because he went to our farm with Bapuji and Kaka.

"I wish you could come with us," Kanubhai said to me before they left. "Without you, the farm will be like a flower without fragrance."

"Bring some peanuts home for me."

"I will. I won't eat a single one there," he said. His voice broke.

I didn't like how Kanubhai's words wavered. Had my widowhood shaken my rock-solid big brother?

I wished I could go to the farm, too. The peanuts had been planted at the beginning of monsoon. In past years I had seen the fields covered with yellow flowers on pealike vines, but I loved it when the rains were gone and the chill set in. It was harvesttime.

Kanubhai used to take me to the farm, and I'd lift a peanut plant, shake away the soil, then pick the fresh pods. Kaka would start a fire and roast some of them right there. At night, when I'd go to sleep, I would smell the rich dark earth and fresh, smoky peanuts.

That evening, Kanubhai returned with the leafy peanut plants. Lakha started a small fire, and I shook the plants to get rid of as much dirt as I could. All of us sat on khatlis surrounding the fire. For the first time since I had become a widow, I could see a smile on Kaka's face as he handed me a few roasted peanuts.

"Did you roast some at the farm?" I asked.

He shook his head. "Why would I? You weren't there."

I wanted to say, "You were all there," but his smile had vanished, so I stayed quiet.

I was eating breakfast in the kitchen when Kanubhai came in holding the newspaper. His face was serious.

"What is it?" I asked

He pointed to an article. "There is a new bill being proposed called the Rowlatt Bill. If it passes, the British sarkar could put anyone in jail. No evidence of wrongdoing would be necessary."

"How can someone be thrown in jail without evidence?" I asked.

Kaki turned toward us. Her face was red from being close to the flame of the stove. "The people in power here sit high above us on a throne. Our hands are not long enough to reach them, but theirs are long enough to reach down to us."

"Gandhiji will fight this. He wrote another article," Kanubhai said, pointing at the paper. "Gandhiji says if the sarkar pushes the Rowlatt Bill, he will declare satyagrah against it."

I remembered how Bapuji had joined the other Kheda farmers and had taken a pledge not to pay taxes. "Will Bapuji join him?"

"He will," Kanubhai said with certainty. "This affects every Indian. We all have to fight."

"Me too?" I asked before I realized what I was doing.

"Yes. Soon it will be time for you to march with everyone."

I had to keep corner for nearly two more months, but one day it would be possible for me to join those men and women. My heart thumped with excitement.

I noticed that Kaki hadn't disagreed with him.

That afternoon, I took Kanubhai's hand in mine and made him sit down next to me.

"Did you talk about me with Bapuji and Kaka?" I asked.

"I tried. . . ."

He looked away before he finished. My voice trembled. "What do you mean by that?"

"It is one thing to discuss, decide, and move on to the next step, but that didn't happen. We kept on going round and round. Bapuji and I were still arguing after two hours."

"What about Kaka?"

"I think he wants to let you go, but Bapuji is so stubborn."

"If I stay here, the rest of my life will be like this year. Instead of keeping corner in our house, I'd be keeping corner in our town. It's not fair that a man can get remarried if his wife dies. Pushpa is Fat Soma's second wife. He didn't have to shave his head and sit in a corner for a year. I had to do that. Now all I am asking is to leave Jamlee so I can do something with my life. Why won't they let me go?"

"Because no other widow from Jamlee has done it."

"Why can't I be the first one who goes away to school? If we are brahman, then nothing can be more important to us than to seek knowledge." My voice wobbled as I said the last sentence.

He focused his attention on me. "Keep up your studies and don't waste your time worrying. Even if Bapuji didn't agree with me, he did listen. It will make sense to him when he thinks about it." He put his hand on my shoulder. "Everything will work out, I promise."

My brother would keep his word. My heart was filled with so many emotions that my words turned into tears.

I threw my arms around his neck. "I'll make you proud."

"I'm already proud of you. Not a day goes by when I'm not thinking about you. In two months you'll be able to go out. You need to be ready. Our people are used to shoving widows in a corner. If you want to be heard, you'll have to be strong, steady, and forceful."

"Like the men and women who march with Gandhiji?"

"Just like them," he said, squeezing my hand.

Kanubhai left early the next morning. When I woke up, it was still dark and cold. I covered myself with a shawl, hurriedly brushed my teeth, and walked back through the chauk to the front steps, where Kaka, Kaki, Ba, Bapuji, and Kanubhai were standing. The darkness was melting, and in a few moments the sky was covered with the golden-red wings of Usha, the goddess of dawn. A mynah bird flew in and out of the tree, singing.

Kanubhai had brought only one cotton bag with two extra pairs of clothes; Ba slipped in a container full of sukhadi, sweets made out of whole-wheat flour roasted in ghee and sweetened with brown sugar, along with a stack of thepla, spicy bread.

I cried as Kanubhai put his hand on my head, on top of my chidri.

Then he turned to Bapuji and Kaka. "Forgive me if I have been rude or stubborn. But only the Lord above knows how this kills me."

I looked at Bapuji and Kaka. Bapuji cleared his throat.

"Take care of yourself," Kaki said. She wasn't crying, but her words still felt wet, as if they had been soaked in tears long before she uttered them.

Every time Kanubhai came, he had to leave. Even though I hated it, I was glad he had come. I cherished the evening we had all spent together in the chauk, with the warmth of the fire, the stream of moonlight, the taste of peanuts. . . . And I was enveloped by the tenderness of my family.

NINETEEN

"FIVE WEEKS left to keep corner," I wrote in my notebook.

I looked in the mirror. With a bald head, brown-ish chidri, and no jewelry, I looked like an ugly doll made from mud. Kanubhai was right. People would look at me and see a widow. They would shun me. All this time I'd waited for the year to end so I could go out, but I wasn't sure anymore.

Now Saviben came twice a week and gave me a lot more homework to prepare for the final exams.

On February sixth, the Rowlatt Bill was introduced at the Imperial Legislative Council in Delhi. Indian leaders opposed it, but it seemed like the sarkar didn't care about their opinions. "Gandhiji is talking about satyagrah against the Rowlatt Bill. Do you think that would make any difference?" I asked Saviben.

"Remember what the Bhagavad Gita says: 'Karmanye vadhikarste ma fuleshu kadachan.' You have the right to fulfill your karma, but not to expect its fruit. Even though we can't predict the sarkar's response, all Indians must oppose this bill, because it is wrong."

"When I study, I expect good marks."

"But if the questions are difficult, you may not do as well. Then you'd be disappointed and frustrated."

"So I should prepare for my exam and not worry about the results?"

"Exactly."

It wasn't easy for me to give up my expectations, though. Maybe that's why I felt the Kheda satyagrah had been a failure, but Gandhiji didn't. He had simply done it because it was his duty to oppose injustice.

After breakfast, I'd quickly scan the headlines from the newspaper because Bapuji wanted to read the paper, too. Then I'd finish my chores, study, and read the paper from cover to cover after lunch. Every day the tension and opposition against the Rowlatt Bill seemed to be mounting.

One day, I saw a letter that Gandhiji had written to the press, telling people about the national school at his ashram. He had expressed his views on education, including the importance of using our mother tongue as the language of instruction, learning Hindi and English, and using the opportunity to study a variety of subjects. He also said that men and women both needed an education if they were going to be equal partners. I liked that.

That afternoon I wrote in my notebook, "Since Bapuji is a follower of satyagrah, will he send me to Gandhiji's ashram to study? Do I really want to go there? I wish Shani were here so we could talk about everything."

I wanted to ask Saviben if she would talk to Bapuji and Kaka about my studies, but I was afraid. What if they argued with her, told her not to interfere in our lives, or worse yet, told her she couldn't teach me anymore?

The winter was waning, and spring warmth began to linger at night. Instead of two blankets, we slept under one. I put away my wool poulkas and thick chidris. We no longer needed to light cow-dung patties and dried twigs to keep warm.

I started counting the days until the year of keeping corner was over. As it got closer and closer, the time seem to go slower and slower, and I became nervous. I paced the corridor in the afternoon while Ba and Kaki napped and Bapuji and Kaka farmed.

The day before the anniversary of Ramanlal's death, Jivima and Heeraben came in the afternoon and sat in the lobby with Kaki and Ba.

"A year has passed, and now Leela doesn't have to keep corner. How fast the year has gone by," Heeraben said.

"The minutes go by slowly, the hours go by quickly, and the years just fly away," said Jivima.

Jivima was wrong. I thought, the widow's first year is like water trapped in a hole, and the shadow of death falls on it. It can't flow. Drop by drop, it drains out.

Kaki glanced at me. "The year has gone slowly for some and faster for others, but it has gone. We must forget it and move on. God is our witness. Our eyes have cried many tears, and our hearts many more. For Leela's sake, let's not cry over spilled fortune."

They were quiet for a while, as if they couldn't think of anything else to say, and then the talk turned to a different subject.

The anniversary of Ramanlal's death came and went.

When I woke up the next day, the eastern sky was as bright as the brick tiles that covered our roof. I heard

Kaki singing *prabhatia*, morning devotional songs. I picked up a fresh stick of acacia to brush my teeth with and walked into the backyard. Lakha greeted me, "*Ram, Ram.*"

"*Ram, Ram, Lakha.*"

I took a deep breath and looked around. The year of keeping corner was over, and everything, the white cottony clouds, the anthill by the back stoop, the kesuda blossoms, and even Dahi and the bullocks looked different.

As I got ready that morning, I thought about my year. It was as if I had been banished from my life, yet I had learned to survive. The first month, Jaya had stayed with me, then Saviben had guided me on the way, and Kanubhai had given me courage.

After I took a bath, Ba gave me a new chidri to wear. New or old, a chidri was a chidri. I didn't even open it. My old one was worn and soft, its colors were a bit faded, and it smelled of our house; the new one was stiff, its colors were too harsh, and it smelled of the chemicals from the cloth mills.

Then I remembered the silk chidri Saviben had brought me. I took it out of the wooden cupboard and wrapped it around myself.

"Do you want to go to the Ramji Mandir?" Kaki asked me.

The temple was right across the street from our house, but I didn't want to go.

That evening I wrote, "Today, the year of keeping corner was over, but I was too scared to even open the front gate and step out. After staying in the house for a year, I'm not sure I'll ever be ready to face the world as a widow."

Saviben came the next morning. "I explained Leela's situation to the school superintendent," she said to Ba. "Leela may take the final exams by herself. I'd like her to take them as soon as possible."

"The year of keeping corner just finished yester-day," Ba reminded her.

"Yes, yes, that is why I'm here."

"Just because the year is over, it doesn't mean Leela needs to go out. Let her take her time—"

"Is Leela ready for the test?" Kaki asked.

In my excitement to take the exams, I forgot my fear of going out. "I'm ready," I said.

Saviben got up. "You can come to school next Wednesday at ten. I'll be there."

I had less than two weeks to prepare.

That night, Ba must have stayed with me until I fell asleep, because all I felt was her hand stroking my back, and then I heard the bells on the bullocks' necks and

Lakha's voice as he led them out from the back gate to the pasture.

The day had begun with fluffy light clouds that gathered like women who gossiped at the well, and then hurried back to their houses after filling their pots. The breeze was neither cold nor warm and came in every few minutes with might.

After I finished my bath, Kaki handed me a silver tray. "Leela, can you get me some flowers for *puja*?"

I hadn't picked flowers for worship since I'd become a widow. I glanced at the garden. It looked strange, a place I'd seen from a window and in dreams but had stepped in only once—on the morning Kanubhai had left. "From the front courtyard?"

"Sooner or later you have to go out, and *shubhasya shikhrum*, the sooner the better."

I walked out barefoot. The winter's cold had made the plumeria drop all its leaves, but now, after a few months, it was full of new, long, waxy ones, and the buds had formed at the end of each cluster. All the rose shrubs were covered with flowers, and there were so many shades of pink roses that I picked more than I needed. The fragrant, white star-jasmines were also blooming.

I didn't put the flowers to my nose and smell them like I would have if I'd picked them for myself. These flowers were for puja, so I wasn't allowed to use them for my own pleasure. Still, the fragrance of all the flowers I'd picked surrounded me.

The hibiscus was brighter than I'd remembered, or maybe I was just used to the duller red of my chidri. I picked all of the hibiscus flowers since they only bloomed for one day.

The garden was so inviting I wanted to linger, but I knew Kaki would be waiting. I went in, gave her the flowers, and asked her if I could study in the garden.

"Go and enjoy, but sit under the shade of the kesuda tree. You haven't been out in the sun, so you need to get used to it slowly."

As I sat on the khatli under the tree, I realized how much I'd missed the front courtyard and the leafy canopy of the kesuda. I watched the sparrows and pigeons going in and out of their nests, feeding their noisy babies. I picked up an orange-red kesuda blossom that had fallen down and put it right in front of me. Then I opened my book and studied.

I was about to go inside when I heard voices coming from the street. I peeked from behind the gate and saw people gathering outside the temple. The faint sound of music came closer. I saw THE RAZAK BAND written on the big drum that a man was carrying, followed by people in white uniforms playing flute, clarinet, and other instruments. The Razak Band was a famous band from the city of Surat, and only the rich could afford to have the group play for them.

Before I knew it, I had opened the gate and stepped out onto the street. From across the street someone shouted, "Aye, Leela, are you crazy? Go, go in the house. No one wants to see the face of a widow before getting married."

It felt as if my feet had sunk into the ground. "Hurry, run in before the groom sees you. It would be a bad omen," someone else said.

Then I heard heavy breathing. I looked up. It was Fat Soma. His eyes were full of fire. He turned toward the people who had told me to go in. "Show some mercy; someday you might need it," he shouted.

Then he whispered, "Chal," and walked me back through the gate.

As soon as we entered the front corridor, I tore away from him, ran to the drawing room, and closed the door. Instead of the band and people's shouts, all I could hear were my own sobs.

A few minutes later Kaki came in and sat beside me. "Fat Soma told me what happened."

I took her hand in mine. I moved her gold bangles up and down her arms so I wouldn't have to look at her.

"Where's Fat Soma?" I asked

"He left."

I stopped playing with her bangles. "Tell me, how can I bring bad luck? I'm just a girl named Leela. What powers do I have? And if I had powers, then wouldn't I have prevented bringing such bad luck to myself?"

"To me you're not bad luck, but other people see you differently. When they see you, they're reminded of what could happen to them or their loved ones, and no one wants to think of it, especially at a happy occasion."

"Fat Soma was widowed once. Why doesn't he bring bad luck?"

"It's different for men. They can marry again and be happy."

"Why can't women be happy again, too?"

She didn't answer.

"Narmad says that women should have the same rights as men. I read an article by Gandhiji that said women and men are equal. So why are people so unfair to widows?"

"I don't know," she said.

If Kaki didn't know the answers, then the only other person I could ask was Saviben, and she wasn't coming until tomorrow. I took out my notebook and wrote, "This morning was a beautiful plumeria blossom, and now it has been trampled. Being a widow means keeping corner for the rest of your life, and I can't let that happen."

TWENTY

AFTER the wedding incident, I studied in the house or backyard.

It had been a month since I'd had a haircut, and my hair was starting to grow back. Each hair was a short stub, but a head full of them had colored my scalp black. When I covered my head with my chidri, it looked like the chidri was floating above my head.

The day before my exams, Nathu came and blanked my scalp again.

Later that afternoon when I was studying, a shadow fell on my book. I looked up at my brother's smiling face.

"Kanubhai!" I gasped. "How did you come in so quietly?" I asked.

"It was you who was studying so diligently that you didn't hear my footsteps."

I closed my book. Now I was too excited to study.

After a dinner of roasted eggplant, yogurt, and rice, we sat in the drawing room.

"Are you ready to take your exams?" Kanubhai asked.

"I am." I wished I could tell him that after my exams I would be ready to go with him. I had to concentrate on my exams, and after they were done I could ask Bapuji for his permission. I didn't want to worry about it now. Maybe someday there would be more on my plate of life, but right now I had to take what I was served.

"Good. I'll walk you to school, unless Bapuji wants to take you." Kanubhai and I both looked at Bapuji, who sat with his lips clamped together.

"You may," Bapuji finally said, staring at the wall. His body was stiff and his eyes were dull. He didn't glance at Kanubhai or me. It seemed to take him so much effort to say even those two words. On Kanubhai's last visit, when we had enjoyed the roasted peanuts, I thought my father and brother had overcome their disagreement. I was wrong. They were just hiding it behind silence. The tension between the two of them was reflected on all our faces.

"Will you stay until Leela's exams are over?" Kaki asked Kanubhai.

"Yes, that's why I came."

My brother had come just for me. This was his fifth visit in one year. I reached for his hand. "I am so happy you're here."

On the first day of my exam, I took a bath, then put on the silk chidri Saviben had given me. Kaki took me to her room. When my eyes adjusted to the darkness, I saw that she had pulled out a wooden *maju*, a trunk, from under the bed. For the past year we hadn't opened the maju, and it was dusty. She wiped it off with a rag.

In the maju was our family's wealth: jewelry and gold bars. A heavy brass *Khambhati* lock made it impenetrable. Kaki took out the silver key chain that was tied to her sari at the waist. She opened the maju and took out a gold hair ornament. It was round with a sturdy gold rod for the back. I was baffled.

"Look at it carefully," she said.

I examined it. One end of the rod was nail-sharp. I still didn't understand. "What should I to do with it?"

"This is for you to keep in your poulka pocket—all the time. If you ever find yourself in danger, don't hesitate to use it. The sharp end will gash your attacker, but it's gold, so it won't infect if you accidentally get scratched."

"Why would anyone attack me?"

She must've seen fear in my eyes, because she pulled me close. "Nothing will happen to you, but as they say, *Chetato nar sada sukhi*, an aware person is a happy person."

Bapuji paced under the kesuda tree, smoking. Kanubhai waited for me there, too. He was dressed in a fresh white dhoti and a shirt.

I felt the flames of heat as I walked out. I hadn't felt that hot for a long time. It was much cooler inside the house, between the mud floor and the clay-tiled roof. Today the breeze was hot and dry, but across from our house the saffron flag at the temple fluttered away just as it did in the cool winds of January.

"May Lord Ganesh take all the obstacles out of your way," Bapuji said to me. Then he added, "Keep your spine and your gaze straight."

Kanubhai and I walked up the narrow, twisty street. We avoided stray dogs, goats, and the stares of curious neighbors who stood in their doorways, saris covering half their faces.

There was Heeraben with her son perched on her hip, pretending to be cleaning her front steps; there was Jivima's daughter-in-law peeking through a window with a rolling pin in her hand; there was Jivima sitting on a wooden swing with her tattered fan. I could picture them all without looking: Heeraben's lips stretched over her protruding gums, Jivima's daughter-in-law's flat nose, Jivima's collapsed jaw, just as clearly as they saw me walking down the street.

I looked at Kanubhai. He kept his head straight. If he hadn't walked with me, would the boys have teased me? Would young girls have twisted their mouths, bunched their eyebrows, and turned away? Maybe they would have just ignored me like I used to ignore widows.

Our street opened onto a big square, into which three other streets also poured. To go to school I had to walk through the main square. Dhiru, who ran a small tea stall, whispered something to his customers, and three or four of them turned around to get a better look at us. Their eyes bit worse than the mosquitoes in monsoon. Jamnadas, the owner of the grocery store, stopped weighing rice for a customer. His eyes met Kanubhai's and then mine. He smiled. "*Beti, shubhantu prasthan*, Daughter, may your journey be good."

Kanubhai waved, and I joined my palms in greeting.

When we reached the school, Saviben met us at the gate. She brought me to her office to take the exam.

Once I started writing the answers, the whole world disappeared and time melted away.

* * *

"Like high tide and low tide, life is full of happiness and sorrow," Kaki used to say.

"After the downpour when the sun comes out, it brings us a rainbow," Ba used to say.

Ever since I had become a widow, Kaki and Ba no longer said those things. But deep within me, a bright vermilion of hope said that maybe the low tide of my life was turning around, that the sun would return to my sky.

Kanubhai walked me to school and back for three days. After the last exam, when we were walking home, he said, "Leela, you're stronger than I thought."

"When you're with me, I'm not afraid."

"All I've done is walk with you, but I can't do it forever. For your safety, always be alert and careful. Don't go out alone at night."

"I won't."

When we came to the banyan tree, I remembered last year. On the way to the fair, Ba had reprimanded me for looking around at people in the market. Today, just the thought of walking past them alone made me shiver.

"How can I ignore what people say?" I mumbled.

He reached out and held my hand. "Remember who you are."

"Leela?"

"No, I mean the real you. You're nothing but pure gold. Does gold change when it's heated and made into different shapes?"

I shook my head.

"It's the same with us. We're all part of the *satchitanand*, true, pure, and blissful consciousness. That's the sum of all the scriptures. No outside influences can change your true self."

Kanubhai's words made me realize that I was definitely not a girl sitting in a corner with a hairless head and wrapped up in the folds of a chidri. I was inside of me.

I had to dive for her like *marjiva*, the pearl divers.

I had only scanned the newspaper while I was studying for my exams, but now I began to read the whole thing again. The Rowlatt Bill was creating a bigger and bigger uproar. People called it "No appeal, no *vakeel*, no *daleel*, no appeal, no lawyer, no argument." Gandhiji met with British officers along with other Indian leaders, wrote letters to the viceroy, and made his opposition clear by addressing people and writing articles to the press. Despite the resistance, the British pushed to pass the bill.

"What will happen now?" I asked Kanubhai,

showing him an article about a protest against the bill. I was sitting on his bed while he packed his bag.

"Gandhiji will declare satyagrah. He has set out rules for it, and people are anxious to follow him."

"The Engrej are big and strong. The Kheda satyagrah didn't make any difference to them. It's like a bee stinging a water buffalo. Nothing will come of it."

"Gandhiji wants all of us to join together. What if hundreds, even thousands of bees attacked the water buffalo? What would happen then?"

I gave him an unblinking look. "That would drive the beast crazy."

We were so absorbed in our conversation that we didn't notice Masi until she said, "Kanubhai, I just heard you were in town so I came to see you."

"It is nice of you to come, but I'm just about to leave," he replied.

"You have no time for your poor masi?"

He gave her a big smile. "Perhaps a few minutes."

With her hands on her hips, Masi declared, "Now that you have finished your studies and Leela is done with keeping corner, you should think about marriage."

He stuffed a shirt in his bag. "Why are you in such a hurry to get me married?"

"It is your responsibility to continue your family's

name. Show me another man in Jamlee who is not married at twenty-two."

"Don't you think I'm special?"

"You are, but what does that have to do with your staying single?"

"If I follow everyone in Jamlee, then I'd be just like them. Every lamb follows blindly. I am a man and make my own decisions." He picked up his bag. "When I decide to get married, you'll be the first one to know."

Masi grinned. "Your sweet talk always melts me."

"I know." He extended his other hand and helped me get up from the bed.

"As soon as I get my results, I'll let you know how I did," I said to him.

"I'll be back before then. That way we can celebrate your success together." He looked at Masi, who was still standing there, and added, "Won't you join us, too?"

Masi was so charmed that she nodded. I wondered if she knew what she was saying yes to.

While I was helping Kaki grind the millet, she said to me, "You've left the house with Kanubhai, and been fine. Tomorrow we'll fetch water together."

I looked at my brass pot. It was covered with dust. For the past year I hadn't touched it, let alone cleaned it.

My pot and I were strangers, like souls separated by many cycles of birth and death. Had someone left in this corner the brass pot that belonged to me in my previous life? A life where Ramanlal was alive, where I wore hibiscus-red and parrot-green, where I roamed the streets with tinkling anklets on my bare feet? I wondered.

I wiped the dust off my pot and shined it by rubbing it with tamarind and ashes from the stove. After I rinsed it, I touched the pot to my cheeks; it felt cool and smooth.

It took Kaki and me a half hour to walk to the well. I tied my pot to a rope and lowered it gently. I wiggled the rope so that the pot would turn on its side and fill with water. It took some time, but Kaki waited patiently. When the pot was full, I used my arms and hands to pull it up. Kaki helped me steady it on the *indhoni*, a ring of soft, padded material that I'd placed on my head.

Right before I'd become a widow, I had been getting better at balancing the full pot, but I hadn't practiced for so long that it felt heavy and wobbly again. That night my arms felt like they were filled with water. I couldn't lift them above my shoulders. Ba massaged oil into them. But I continued bringing water home every day so my arms could get used to it. After a week, it was easy to wiggle the rope and balance the pot on my head.

Once my arms stopped hurting, I started grinding the millet and wheat by myself. Without Kaki helping me, the elephant-heavy stone seemed impossible to turn. I could grind only a handful at first, but added a little more every day. I could feel strength in my arms from the muscles that were getting as thick as rope.

Ever since Shani had left, I swept and mopped the floor, and my legs grew strong from squatting. But they were never as strong as my hands. And I knew that women like Shani, who wore heavy anklets and bracelets, had even stronger legs and arms.

One day Ba went to Fat Soma's house because Pushpa was sick. When Ba returned, she said, "I'm no doctor, but Pushpa's cheeks are as red as watermelon flesh, and the whites of her eyes look tough as rind. Those are signs of the sickness riding her body. Besides, tonight is an unlucky night, the fourteenth day of the vanishing moon, a dangerous time for the sick and the old."

"Who knows, she may sit up and be fine tomorrow. When kismet and karma play, we're nothing but pawns in their game," Kaki said, picking up her prayer beads. I knew she was going to pray for Pushpa.

Late that night, Fat Soma returned carrying a lantern and asked Kaki and Ba to come with him. His eyes were swollen and webbed with red. I remembered how instead of eating a penda, he had wrapped it in his handkerchief to take to Pushpa. He loved her very much. And then I thought about Ramanlal. I wondered if he'd loved me even though we'd never lived together.

Pushpa's condition worsened during the night, and she passed away the next day.

It was the day I read in the newspaper that the Rowlatt Bill had passed.

Saviben came by that afternoon. Ba offered her tea, but she politely refused, saying, "I wanted to say good-bye to Leela. I have resigned my post and am leaving for Ahmedabad to work with Gandhiji."

My heart sank. "So I won't see you anymore?"

"I hope you'll come to Ahmedabad to visit me. Besides, I'll be back when your results come."

As she walked out, her white sari palav got caught in the wooden gate. She pulled it gently. It reminded me of when she first came to teach me and had to tug her palav from me.

I wrote in my notebook, "No matter how far Saviben goes, she will always be with me."

Ever since the Rowlatt Bill had passed, there were many articles by Indian leaders denouncing it. Gandhiji had said, "The Rowlatt Bill has affected me deeply. I'll decide my course shortly. I can no longer render obedience to a power that is capable of such devilish legislation. Satyagrah will be my route. I invite all to join me."

There were large gatherings and protests in Delhi, Amritsar, Mumbai, Madras, and other cities. Since Gandhiji lived in Ahmedabad, the city was always in the news. The country was looking to him for guidance, and despite his delicate health, he was crisscrossing India to urge and organize a nationwide protest.

Gandhiji announced April sixth as the date for observance of humility and prayers. He urged people to go on *hartal*, strike, and protest peacefully against the Rowlatt Bill. It was only two weeks away.

Were we ready for it?

TWENTY-ONE

A FEW DAYS later, Heeraben strode in with her sari going *swish-swoosh, swish-swoosh,* like it wanted to spill out a secret. "There is talk about arranging a new marriage for Fat Soma," she said to Ba and Kaki.

"My cousin's son?" Ba asked.

"Yes. Is there another Fat Soma in town?" She took a pinch of tobacco from Kaki's tobacco box. "Not yet nineteen, and this will be his third wedding. Poor boy!"

If Fat Soma was a poor boy, what about his wife, Pushpa? Didn't she deserve to be called unfortunate because she died so young? True, Fat Soma was devastated, but at least he didn't have to keep corner, shave his head, and wear widower's clothes. I wondered how he felt about people talking about a new marriage two weeks after Pushpa had died.

The next afternoon, when Ba, Kaki, and I were sitting in the corridor, Fat Soma came to visit. Ba spread a mat for him to sit on. Kaki took a long sniff of her tobacco and asked how he was.

"I've been busy."

"Busy with getting married again?" Ba asked.

Fat Soma's face turned grim. I cringed.

He shook his head as if to get rid of his sadness. "A group of *sadhus* have been staying at Lord Shiva's temple for weeks now. I've been helping those holy men."

All at once Kaki's eyes were on Fat Soma as if he had revealed a secret.

Fat Soma turned to me. "Are you going back to school?"

"I'm done with school here, but I want to continue," I said, and looked at Ba and Kaki.

Fat Soma eyes brightened. His crooked tooth poked out a bit. "That'll be good for you. What do you want to study?"

"I can become a teach—"

Before I could finish, Ba said, "Clamp your mouth, Leela. We have not talked about this."

No one said anything for a while, but Fat Soma didn't leave. So I offered him some tea.

Ba fried some dried kothimda slices while I made the tea. She sprinkled them with salt, red pepper, and lime juice. The last time I'd had kothimda was at Ramanlal's house. The thought made me choke up, so I hardly ate any. The slices were paper-thin and the size of a silver rupee. Ba and Kaki had only a half dozen each, but Fat Soma finished all of them, as if he were not going to eat for a long time.

After we'd finished eating and drinking, Fat Soma leaned against the wall cross-legged. He kept tapping his fingers on the mat and looking from me to Kaki to Ba.

Kaki asked him, "Is there anything you wish to tell us?"

"No, no. It's time for me to say good-bye and get your blessing."

He got up and bowed to Kaki. "May you find peace," she said to him.

What kind of blessing was that? I thought. Most of the time when elders blessed someone they said, "May you live a hundred years," or "May you be prosperous and happy," but never "May you find peace." That always came later in life, and often after the life was no more. It was a blessing for a soul.

When he bent his head down to Ba, she said, "You don't have to bow down every time you come for a visit. It's not like you're going on a long journey."

"A blessing is something I can always use."

"You're right," she said. "May you be the father of five fine sons," she said.

He smiled, but there was something in Fat Soma's eyes that made me think he was humoring her. It was as if he hadn't exactly accepted her blessing, but was amused by it instead.

When I said good-bye to him, he whispered, "Don't let anyone stop you from studying. We must all find our own paths."

The next day there was a commotion in town. Fat Soma had disappeared during the night. He'd taken off his janoi and left it with a note, saying, "I've renounced the world. Do not try to find me."

When Fat Soma's father and a few other relatives went to the station, they heard that the group of sadhus had left for Kashi early in the morning. His bapuji and uncle followed them.

I wondered if they'd find Fat Soma, and if they would be able to bring him back. If Fat Soma had renounced the world, it meant he'd severed his connection with his father, mother, and all his other relatives. He wouldn't be attached to any possessions and wouldn't be bound by any mundane *dharma*, duty, to people who lived in society. He would have no caste, no family, no society to answer to. His sole purpose would be to seek *moksha*, nirvana. It was possible that the deaths of his first wife, his friend Ramanlal, and Pushpa made him realize that life was full of suffering. Like the Buddha, he had decided to take this path to find peace.

Fat Soma, as I knew him, was no more.

That night under the kesuda tree, men sat on the khatlis and women sat in the front corridor.

"Fat Soma will be home in a day or two," Masi said. "It is easy to run away, but it is not easy to be a sadhu. As soon as his bapuji finds him and twists his ear, he will come to his senses."

"What if no one can find him?" I asked.

Heeraben said, "With a name like Fat Soma, people will remember him, and his bapuji will have no problem spotting him."

"He may change his name. Fat Soma was his worldly name," I said.

Masi waved her hand. "Not Fat Soma. He was too attached to his name."

"I agree," said Heeraben.

"If he had left everyone and everything to become a sadhu, why would he keep his old name? Once he changes his name and wears a saffron robe, he will blend in with all the other sadhus," I said.

"Leela might be right," Kaki said. "With the hartal coming up, it'll be impossible to find him, especially if he has reached Kashi and is on his way to the Himalayas. His relatives might not be able to follow him."

Masi said, "The hartal day will come and go like any other day."

Kaki gave me a glance, then said, "Don't be so sure. Unity and national pride are changing our country."

Masi fell quiet, but Heeraben did not. "I say a few people in Ahmedabad will listen to Gandhiji and not go to work, but the whole country will not. Who would want to make the Engrej angry?"

"That is the plan," I said. "Because of the hartal, no one will show up for work in the big cities. All the factories, colleges, and offices will be closed."

Heeraben got up, saying, "Even if the city people go on hartal, it won't matter much in Jamlee."

"Not at all," Masi chimed in.

Heeraben and Masi were wrong. On April sixth, Bapuji and Kaka stayed home, and by the late morning, many men had gathered under our kesuda tree.

Ba looked out and said, "All this agitation worries me."

"Why?" I asked.

"Because no one can keep a crowd under control. If the sarkar arrest Gandhiji, Ahmedabad will be the first place where things could go wrong."

"What can happen?"

"Plenty," she said, pointing to the men gathered in our front yard. "In the city, the same crowd would be a hundred times bigger, and if a fight with the police erupted, it would take less than three breaths before people were hurt or killed."

Even though I wanted to hear what the men were saying in the front courtyard, I stayed inside. I didn't want Ba to see how interested I was.

In the middle of the turmoil, we received one pleasant piece of news. Shani wrote me a three-line letter telling me she'd had a baby girl and that both of them were doing well. Lakha was already with Shani and the baby. I hoped all three of them would return soon.

I read in the newspaper that on the day of the hartal, Gandhiji addressed people on Chowpatty Beach in Mumbai. The place was full of men and women, and there were some children there, too. The crowd looked like a giant wave. He denounced the Rowlatt Act as the *Kalo Kaydo*, Black Law.

I wished I could have been there.

Also on that day, the entire country, from one end to the other, towns as well as villages, observed a complete hartal. The people filled the streets as if they were celebrating a holiday. It was spectacular.

The next evening, Gandhiji and the volunteers sold

two books in the streets of Mumbai. Both were written by Gandhiji: *Hind Swaraj, Indian Self Rule*, and *Sarvodaya*, a Gujarati adaptation of John Ruskin's book of social criticism, *Unto This Last*. This was to show civil disobedience. Both books had been banned by the government, and people had been warned that they could be arrested and jailed if they bought them.

People paid four times, ten times, twenty times the cost. All the money Gandhiji raised was going to be used for future demonstrations of civil disobedience.

That night I floated in and out of my dreams. I was riding a wave. People covered every inch of the beach, policemen rode on horses, and even though I had never heard Gandhiji's voice, it echoed all around me.

Later in the week, just as it looked like things were quieting down, Bapuji and Kaka came home late from the farm with grim faces. Bapuji took off his turban and wiped his forehead. "Gandhiji teaches us nonviolence, and what do people do when they find out he is arrested? They become violent."

I gasped. "Is Gandhiji in jail?"

"No, they let him go. But people are rioting."

"Where? In Ahmedabad? Mumbai? Delhi?"

"When we stopped to get bidis, Jamnadas told us that people have gone wild in Ahmedabad."

"How does he know?" Ba asked, handing him a glass of water.

Bapuji drank the water. "Jamnadas just returned from the city this afternoon. There are also rumors that rioting is going on in other places. Here in Jamlee, those two men who took our animals were beaten."

"They were horrible," I said, remembering how one had hit Dahi. "Mani died because of them."

"It doesn't matter. Nonviolence means you must show restraint."

Bapuji was right.

I had counted on Kanubhai to convince Bapuji to let me go with him to study. Now I realized that Kanubhai might not be able to travel from Ahmedabad in the middle of all the turmoil.

I thought about talking to Bapuji myself, but in light of what was happening, this was not a good time.

The wave of uncertainty and change that had swept the whole country could crush my dream.

TWENTY-TWO

MY HEART pounded with anticipation when I opened the paper in the morning. Ba was right. Even Gandhiji couldn't control people's emotions and actions. He was in Mumbai when a mob in Ahmedabad burned down the telegraph and collector's office. When Gandhiji heard about it, he cried. He returned to the ashram immediately, and miraculously was able to restore peace.

Kaki had gone to visit her brother for a week, so it was only Kaka, Bapuji, Ba, and me in the house. One afternoon Ba and I sat on a cotton rug sipping sweetened buttermilk. That morning Ba had washed her hair with aritha fruit, and it had a fresh fruity, smell. Her hair spread out over her back and brushed the rug. It was the perfect time to talk to her.

"My results will come soon," I said.

"Yes. You'll pass."

"I know that. I want to become a teacher or a doctor."

Ba gave me a lingering look.

I straightened up. "Isn't it our dharma to learn and impart knowledge? The great sage Vashista's wife, Arundhati, and Agasya's wife, Lopamudra, were learned women. Didn't they teach and discuss philosophy with other learned men and women?"

"You're a widow."

"Gandhiji thinks widows should be able to go to school. Narmad said the same thing fifty years ago. What good are all their ideas if widows and their families don't take the lead? Ba, I want to study, and I need your help."

Ba took a long sip of her buttermilk. Some of it stuck to her upper lip.

I took her hand in mine. "Do I have your blessing?"

"How can I let you go alone?"

I moved closer to her and ran my fingers through her moist, gleaming hair. "I won't be alone. There are boarding schools for students who don't live at home. Gandhiji is starting one at his ashram, too. I can study there. And Kanubhai and Saviben will be there."

Ba took a deep breath. "What about your bapuji?"

My heart sank. "I'm not sure."

"We have to think about how to talk to your bapuji," she said as we sipped our buttermilk slowly.

Sometimes I didn't understand why Ba had to spill every detail of our lives to Masi. The day after Ba and I talked, Masi hurried through the corridor. Giving me a hasty look, she went to the kitchen. I followed.

"The whole town is talking about Leela going to Ahmedabad to study," Masi said to Ba.

"How did they find out?" I asked.

Ba stopped cutting carrots. "Yes, how did they?" she echoed.

"Well, when I told Heeraben, Jivima's daughter-in-law was standing right there with a couple of other women and—"

"So you told half the town." I chuckled.

Masi picked up a carrot and took a bite.

"Even if people talk, we have to do what's right," Ba said. "Today things are done on a piece of paper, and people sign it. Houses and farms change masters that way. Mind you, they sign it; they don't just put their thumbprint on it. They read what's written on that piece of paper and understand it, and in the future, Leela will need to understand all that. Otherwise she'll see no difference between black letters and black ants."

"These are not your ideas," Masi said to Ba. "These are Kanubhai and Leela's ideas. In the old times, children obeyed their parents and did what they were told. It seems that your children tell *you* what to do. Have womenfolk ever needed to study? What use are black letters to us? And if Leela needs to learn, who better than her bapuji and kaka to teach her right here at home?" She took another bite of her carrot.

"Leela needs to study."

I couldn't believe Ba had said that. She must have been thinking about it for many months now.

"You'll be sorry if you send her away," Masi said.

"Leela needs to study," Ba repeated. Her voice was tired and chewed-up as if she had mulled over the idea a thousand times.

"If that's your mantra," Masi said, "I've nothing more to say."

She picked up another carrot and left without saying good-bye.

When Bapuji and Kaka came home, they took quick baths, then Bapuji sat down for his evening meditation. I heard the Gayatri Mantra that he recited every morning and evening.

Om. The glory of that Savitur (the universal energy),
Most brilliant!
On that divine radiance, let me meditate;
May it inspire me with excellent understanding.

I prayed for Bapuji and me to have excellent under-standing.

With each other.

I was almost asleep when I heard Ba say, "Leela, the sun will set soon. Let's eat and clean the kitchen before it gets dark."

"*Aavee*, coming."

I laid down four *patla*, low wooden stools, for us to sit on. Ba dished out our food. She gave the first plate to Kaka, the second to Bapuji, and the third to me. She served herself last. Bapuji poured milk from the brass jug into our glasses.

A thought rose in my head. Now that Masi had spread the word, what if someone asked Bapuji about my going to Ahmedabad? If that happened, he would be furious with me and Ba.

I had to talk to Bapuji, but I was so afraid he'd refuse. If he said no, there would be nothing left for me. Maybe it was better not to say anything; that way I could keep on dreaming.

"What's the matter, Leela? Your ba made your favorite food and you're eating like a sparrow. Aren't you hungry?" Bapuji asked.

"I'm eating."

My words came out as thick as buffalo milk. It felt like my heart was in my throat. I focused my gaze on my plate as I broke off a piece of millet bread and scooped up curried spinach with it. I managed to stuff it in my mouth and chew, but I couldn't swallow. My throat had no room for any food. I took a big gulp of milk and forced it all down.

"She'll start eating when her kaki comes back," Ba said.

Kaka put his calloused palm on my shoulder and said, "Eat in peace and the food will turn into blood, eat in agony and it will turn into poison."

After supper, Kaka and Bapuji smoked bidis in the courtyard and I helped Ba clean the kitchen. A few other men gathered under the tree, and I prayed no one would talk about me. My mind still couldn't settle down. I wished Kaki were home. It would be easier to talk to Bapuji with her, Kaka, and Ba on my side.

Then I thought of Masi. If I waited, she might fill Ba's head with stories about widows like Kaveri.

I was so engrossed in my thoughts that I accidentally spilled the ashes from the stove. A dark cloud rose. I began coughing, and my eyes stung. "Go," Ba said. "I'll finish up."

I walked out of the kitchen and stood in the front doorway as the last of the sunlight mixed with the dust rising from the pounding of animal hooves. I listened to the symphony of the temple bells, drums, and cymbals that were ringing all over the town for the evening aarti. The prayer from the Ramji Mandir filled the air.

The evening cooled the earth but it couldn't cool me.

Darkness came swiftly, and Ba lighted a lamp. "Jai Shri Krishna," she said.

"Jai Shri Krishna," I echoed.

Bapuji and Kaka came inside. Kaka went to bed, but Bapuji, Ba, and I sat in the chauk. I lay my head in Ba's lap and spread my body on the stone floor. Gently, she began stroking my head. It was a clear night, and I admired the plain blue sky of the day dressed in a beautiful star-studded sari. If only I had courage to talk to Bapuji, then I could make my life turn that beautiful.

Bapuji and Ba were discussing what to plant, and I must have fallen asleep in her lap, because when I woke up, the seven-point Saptarshi had moved in the sky. I heard Bapuji say to Ba, "What's the use of sending Leela to school?"

I lay as still as a crouching tiger so they wouldn't suspect that I was hunting their talk.

"Leela wants to go to school. We're her parents, and it's our dharma to help her achieve her goal," Ba said.

"I refuse to send her so far away."

"Jamlee can offer Leela nothing. Kanubhai can take her to Ahmedabad. If she stays in one of the boarding schools, she'll have supervision."

"We won't be there."

"We can't be with her for the rest of her life. She needs to learn to take care of herself. She's a smart girl and she can make a new life for herself. I can't watch her suffering like this."

"The year is over. She can go out."

"You know Leela—"

He cut her off, saying, "She doesn't know what is good for her. We are done talking about this subject forever."

Ba sighed. I felt the warmth of her breath on my ears.

Bapuji had forbade Ba from discussing it again. She would respect that and not say a word.

I had to talk to Bapuji. Soon.

TWENTY-THREE

I WOKE UP EARLY the next morning and couldn't go back to sleep. I felt that I'd lose my courage if I waited until evening to talk to Bapuji.

As soon as Bapuji was done with his bath, I asked him, Kaka, and Ba to come to the drawing room. When they sat down, I stood in front of them and said, "My results will be out soon and I'm sure I'll get good marks. I want to be a teacher or a doctor. Since I can't do that in Jamlee, I would like your permission to study in Ahmedabad."

"O, Rama," Kaka said, shaking his head as if nothing good was going to come out of this conversation.

I hadn't expected that response from Kaka. "Is it wrong for me to ask?"

"It isn't," he replied.

I looked at Bapuji. His large forehead shone in the morning light, making him look like a wise sage.

"You have the right to ask, but we have the right to refuse," Bapuji said.

"Please, listen to me," I said. "Before I became a widow, I never thought about studying, but the past year has taught me a lot. Being a widow is worse than anything I could have ever imagined. If I don't make something out of myself, I'll be nothing but a widow for the rest of my life. I don't want that."

"It is your kismet," said Bapuji.

"Maybe being a widow is my kismet, but that doesn't mean I have to suffer for the rest of my life. It wasn't my fault that Ramanlal died. If you send me to Ahmedabad, I'll work hard and make you proud. I'll be able to help people, the way Saviben helped me. My life won't be wasted." I said all this so fast that I had to stop and take a deep breath. Bapuji didn't let me continue.

"I have argued enough with your brother about this, and I don't wish to do that with you," he said.

Ba's lips were sealed.

This was it. I was going to stay in Jamlee for the rest of my life. I would be known as a child widow, bearer of bad luck, shunned from celebration, banished to a corner for the rest of my days. I couldn't let this talk die before it had even started. I didn't realize I was trembling until Kaka pointed to a seat next to him and said, "Come, sit by me."

He put his hand on my shoulder and gave it a little squeeze. I looked at him, and he nodded slightly and whispered, "Go on."

I wished I'd prepared my arguments and thought this through. My hands turned clammy and my throat was dry. But the time was now. I swallowed hard and gathered my courage. "Bapuji, when you joined the Kheda satyagrah, you said you wouldn't pay the taxes even if the sarkar arrested you and locked you up."

"I did."

"Was it because it was the right thing to do?"

"Yes."

"You also participated in the hartal by staying home. I think it took courage to fight against the sarkar." I took a deep breath and continued, "Did you break the law because you agree with Gandhiji's ideas of higher truth?"

"Don't loop your talks," Bapuji said. "What does this have to do with you?"

"You've been reading the newspapers, and you know that Gandhiji considers women equal to men and wants to start a school for boys and girls."

"I disagree with Gandhiji on that point. Fighting the

sarkar is one thing and breaking tradition is another. They have nothing in common."

It was difficult to tell Bapuji that he was wrong without sounding disrespectful. I lowered my voice. "They do. Following the truth is the same, whether it is against the foreign government or our own society. It requires courage. It's easier to follow customs than to question them. Bapuji, we have to take a pledge to fight against all that is wrong and cruel, including customs and prejudices. Don't our scriptures, *Vedas*, say that truth is whole? So how can we fragment it? How can we fight against cruelty and unfairness in some cases but not in others? I didn't do anything wrong, but I have to suffer. Fat Soma's wife died, but he did not suffer. Don't I have a right to wage satyagrah against that?"

I waited for Bapuji's reply, but he was silent. Was he angry with me, or had my words reached his heart?

Finally, Kaka said to Bapuji, "I'll not tell you what you should do. You must search your heart and make the decision, but what Leela says has the soul of the Vedas in it."

"Yes," Bapuji said. I wondered what was going through his mind. Then he stood up. "Leela, Kanubhai fought for you, but he couldn't convince me that your going away to school was a good idea. You made me realize that this is not just about you, it is also about something bigger." Then he turned to Kaka. "If Leela has your blessing, she can go to Ahmedabad."

"May you become as learned as Arundhati," Kaka said, wrapping his arm around me.

I saw Ba wipe tears as Bapuji put his hand on my head.

TWENTY-FOUR

THE HEAT of summer had sucked the last drop of juice from the soil. The air stood still and heavy as if it were lonely. But the lush mango trees were laden with fruit.

In the morning, while Ba took a bath, I fed Dahi and the bullocks and then set off to get drinking water. I wanted to finish the chores before Kaki came back so we would have time to sit and talk. After crossing the market at Chokdi, where four roads met, I walked faster. I was late today, and as far as I could see there was no one on the path.

I'd almost passed an abandoned shed when I heard some noises. Suddenly, the wall came alive. One hand grabbed me and yanked me behind the wall, and the other covered my mouth. My pot fell and I stumbled. The hands were strong. They pushed me in the corner tight against the wall.

The man wore a scarf around his mouth and had his head tied with a scarf, too, so all I could see were his eyes and nose. With one hand he pushed my hands behind my back, and with the other he pulled at my chidri. I'd tucked it tightly, and while he struggled with it, I wiggled my arm free. I dipped my hand in my poulka pocket and grabbed the *khilli* that Kaki had given me. Then I attacked my attacker. With all the force I had, I dragged the sharp end of it on his arm. It dug deep into his skin, which bled. Shocked, he took a step back.

"Raand," he cursed, and rushed toward me. He tried to grab the khilli away, but I went for his eyes, and he backed off. So I scratched his other hand instead, and blood began to drip out of it, too. He fled. I stood there shaking like a baby sparrow in a thunderstorm.

I walked home with my empty pot.

What Masi said about men taking advantage of women came rushing back to me. It had made me mad then, but now I realized there was truth in what she had said. Masi wanted me to be safe. She didn't want me to end up like Kaveri, cut off from her family, friends, and hometown.

The man brought back the memory of the kalotar I had seen. At least I could tell Bapuji about the kalotar and he could get rid of it. Nothing could be done about this human snake.

When I got home, Kaki was there. Tears streamed down my face as I told her and Ba what had happened. Ba stared up at the sky and said, "God was with you."

"Yes. God was with her, and her courage was with her, too," Kaki said.

"I'm afraid that if he'd been a bigger, stronger man, I wouldn't have been able to defend myself."

My confidence had evaporated. As I lay in my bed that night, clutching my pillow, I couldn't believe I was the same girl who had convinced Bapuji to let me go to Ahemdabad the day before. Was I ready to go out in the world?

When Nathu came to cut my hair, I heard him say to Bapuji, "Looks like the monsoon is going to come early. You'll need to plow and seed in a few weeks."

"I'll need help, then. As you go around today, can you ask Batuk the tailor, his brother, and your brother to come?"

"I'll ask them, but I don't think Batuk can do it."

"Why not? Is he very busy?"

"No, no, it's not the work. He's hurt himself. God knows how, but he's scratched both his arms badly."

I felt as if a snake had slithered across my back.

"Leela, sit still, or you might get hurt," Nathu said.

The name and the face of my attacker were no longer a mystery.

I had passed Batuk's tailor shop on the way to get water. He must've seen me walking alone that morning, and planned his attack. The thought of it filled me with a stinging of anger and fear. I vowed to always stay alert and fit. My life depended on it.

That night, when I lay down again, I couldn't fall asleep. I got up twice to drink water.

"What is the matter?" Kaki asked.

"I know who attacked me."

"Who?"

"It was Batuk," I whispered.

I could hear her gasp. "I had a feeling."

"Why? Has he tried to rape other girls?"

"In a small town like Jamlee, it's easy to know everyone's reputation, although no one has come out and accused Batuk."

"Why?"

"Because they are afraid it would taint the victim more than Batuk."

"That makes no sense."

Kaki shook her head. "Sadly, that's how it is. You're leaving in a few days and need your rest. Go to bed now," she said. "You'll feel better in the morning."

It was easy to close my eyes, but it was impossible to shut out the world.

There was something terribly wrong with what Kaki had said, and I trembled with anger. I couldn't understand how the people of Jamlee tolerated men like Batuk. They should have been enraged. They should have wanted to protect their sisters and daughters from him. Instead, they were silent. We had a saying that when people don't have the courage to stand up against injustice, they "shield their eyes with their ears." That way they can pretend nothing is wrong, and they let the victims suffer. By ignoring such brutality, people were just as guilty as Batuk and others like him. I hid my face in the pillow and cried.

TWENTY-FIVE

IN THE WINTER I loved to pull the silky *rajai* up to my chin and sleep for a few extra minutes, but in the summer I flung away my thin covers as soon as I woke up. Today I stayed in bed for a long time. My happiness had dissolved. My dreams of studying in Ahmedabad frightened me now. I thought about what I should do.

There was only one path. If I let the fear and anger get stronger, it would weaken me. I had to turn off my terror and snuff my rage.

In one of the poems by Narmad, there was a line: *Ya hom karine pado, fateh che agay,* jump in with gusto and success is ahead. I repeated it to myself.

That afternoon my mood changed unexpectedly. I was putting away leftover food from lunch when I heard, "Leelabon, we're home."

I ran out of the kitchen and saw Shani in the chauk

with her baby. She handed her daughter to me and said, "I've been waiting for you to bless her."

In Jamlee, people avoided widows, and yet Shani was asking me to bless her child. I took the baby in my arms and said, "May you live a long life."

"Bless her to be a pundit like you."

"I'm no pundit," I said, "but may your daughter be a pundit *shiromani!*"

"What's a shiromani?"

"Pundit shiromani is the person pundits consult if they have questions."

"Are you a shiromani?"

"Not at all," I said. By that time, Ba and Kaki had come out, and I handed the baby to Kaki.

Later, Shani came over again. She brought her slate and her baby. "Are you ready?" she asked as she sat cross-legged with the baby on her lap and the slate in her hand. "You'll be so proud of me. I haven't forgotten a single thing."

My heart ached. How was I going to tell her that I'd only be able to teach her for a few more days? I avoided looking at her. "Then let's begin."

She put the slate down. "Don't you want to teach me, Leelabon?"

"I do, but I have to tell you something. I am leaving Jamlee soon."

She grabbed my wrist. "You're going to Ahmedabad? To study?" Her eyes and smile were wide.

It made me relax. "Why are you so happy that I'm going away? I thought you'd miss me," I teased.

Her face turned serious. "I will miss you. But your joy is my joy, and it is this big," she said, spreading her arms wide.

Kanubhai arrived the next day.

I was chopping almonds in the kitchen when he came in. He looked around. "Where are Ba and Kaki?" he asked.

"Ba is doing laundry, and Kaki is doing her puja."

"Saviben told me that your results will come in a day or two," he said.

I was puzzled. "How did—"

"Don't forget, we both live in the same city. I met her at the ashram."

"Will you take me back with you?" I asked.

"Bapuji still has to let you go."

"I have Bapuji's permission."

His eyes brightened. "It's a miracle, Leela. It is simply a miracle."

I told Kanubhai that I had spoken to Bapuji because Masi's visit had left me without a choice. I told him how Kaka had encouraged me in his quiet way, and how I was able to change Bapuji's mind.

When we were done talking, I said, "I'm ready to go."

"You certainly are."

"Leela, are you done chopping almonds?" I heard Ba's voice.

I was so absorbed in talking to Kanubhai that I had stopped working.

I picked up an almond and a knife.

He picked up a handful of almonds. "Less work for you," he whispered, and put a few in his mouth.

"Almost done, Ba," I said.

Later that day, I went to the farm with Kanubhai and Bapuji. As the three of us strode around, Bapuji talked about when he was planning to plow and what he was planning to grow. Kanubhai didn't ask him about my studies then or even later that night while we ate a dinner of curried squash, *bajari* bread, and thick buffalo milk yogurt.

It was a clear night and the half-moon shone brightly. If you looked carefully, you could see the darkened other half, too. Since it was getting warmer, Lakha had put three khatlis out for Ba, Kaki, and me in the chauk. The three of us and Kanubhai sat there talking.

"School doesn't start for a few more weeks, but I want to take Leela to Ahmedabad with me now. So she'll get used to the city," Kanubhai said.

"I'll miss her, but I have to let her go. Jamlee can offer her nothing else, and there's a whole world out there," Ba replied. Then she added, "In the past year Leela has taught me a lot."

"What have you learned from me?" I wondered aloud.

"You have shown us what courage is," Kaki said.

The other two nodded in agreement.

Ba said to Kanubhai, "Now that you have kept your own promise, will you—"

Kanubhai raised his hand and stopped Ba from finishing her sentence. "Not a word about that."

I had no idea what they were talking about.

Ba put her arm around me and pulled me close. "In Ahmedabad, people are following Gandhiji, and every day there are marches and protests, and you'll be right in the middle of it. What if you get involved?"

"I only want to study."

"You will be involved," she said. "Just be careful."

I snuggled up closer. "I will."

On the day my exam results came, a hot wind was blowing but my heart danced like a blade of grass in the monsoon—fresh and eager. Saviben came dressed in a khadi sari. Her face beamed.

"You came back!" I said, and rushed to her.

"I'm here with your results," she said.

We all gathered in the drawing room, including Shani, Lakha, and the baby. Saviben waited until we sat down. "Leela, you scored the highest marks in the district." She held out some papers to me and added, "You won a scholarship. As soon as you sign these forms, I can release the money."

My eyes widened. "I got a scholarship?"

"Yes, and I'm so happy you'll be able to use it."

I wanted to thank her, hug her, tell her what she meant to me.

I was speechless.

I looked at my family. No one said a word, but their glowing eyes and proud faces said everything I needed to hear.

When I handed the signed paper back to Saviben, she said, "Leela, Mrs. Mistry is one of the education inspectors. She's known me since I was a baby. If you ever need any help, don't hesitate to contact her."

"I won't."

Kaki invited Saviben for lunch, but she was in a hurry. When I bowed to her, she said, "May learning bring joy to your life."

My guru's blessing was the most important one I could have before I went on to learn new things. There were unknown dangers that would cross my path, hiding in the pleats of saris, in the turn of turbans, in the unknown eyes of the city, but the blessings of my elders would always guard me.

I walked Saviben to the gate. "There's something I must tell you," she whispered. "It has to do with your brother."

"Kanubhai?"

"When you were first widowed, he came to me and asked me to tutor you. I was new in town and afraid of what people would say. I argued that it would do no good to teach you for one more year. There was no school beyond that in town, and your parents would never send a widow away to study."

"What did he say?"

"He promised me that you'd keep studying. I said, 'It's easier to make promises than fulfill them. Once you're married, you'll forget about it.' And that's when he told me he wouldn't get married until you were allowed to continue your education."

All the talks I'd had with Kanubhai flooded my mind. And what had he told Bapuji and Kaka under the kesuda tree? What had he said to Ba and Kaki? My heart, throat, and eyes swelled up with love for my brother. "Why?" I cried.

"So you could have your life back. You're lucky

to have him. Not many brothers would do that."

"Yes, I'm lucky."

After Saviben left, I went to the kitchen. Ba was taking out mango pulp, and Kaki was making two-layered rotli.

"May I roll out the last few rotli?" I asked Kaki.

"Do it. After today you won't get a chance to do it for a long time."

I took two dough balls and dusted them with flour. Stacking one on top of the other, I flattened them, rolled them out together, then cooked them on the sagdi. The coal beneath it was burning bright. After the rotli was cooked, and while it was still hot, I pulled apart the two layers. The trapped steam rose. Rotli made like this was whisper-thin.

I told Ba and Kaki about my conversation with Saviben. "Did Kanubhai really refuse to marry until you let me study?"

Ba didn't reply.

"Why didn't you tell me?"

"Because we promised him we wouldn't. We couldn't break that promise, could we?" Kaki said.

I wondered what other things were done and said without my knowledge. What other sacrifices were made, and by whom, for me?

That afternoon, Heeraben told Ba that some parents were very angry. They said that I had an advantage since Saviben had tutored me last year. Some even said that I probably knew the questions before the exams and had prepared my answers.

I laughed. "You know the saying, 'Let the ghost of gossip appear. It can't scare the truth.'"

The rest of the day slipped from my hand so swiftly that I wrote down in my notebook, "Happy times are light and fast, sad times are heavy and slow. They all end, though, and what remains is me. Just me."

I woke up late the next morning and saw all my family sitting in the chauk. Their faces looked like they had seen a kalotar.

"What happened?" I asked.

"Something terrible," Kanubhai replied, pointing to the newspaper. "A few days ago, following the orders of General Dyer, police opened fire on the people in Amritsar at the Jallianwala Bagh."

"Were they rioting?"

"No, they'd gathered peacefully to listen to political speeches. Many were villagers from surrounding areas who'd come to celebrate *Baisakhi*."

Baisakhi was a spring festival. I could imagine people dressed in vibrant colors of kesuda and mustard blossoms milling around. My voice shook. "Did anyone die?"

"Leela, more than a thousand rounds were fired without warning, without telling the people to leave. Hundreds, maybe thousands, are dead or injured."

I covered my face.

"Men, women, children. Sikhs, Hindus, Muslims."

I closed my eyes. Innocent people mowed down, like blades of grass.

I didn't bother to get ready or eat my breakfast, but read the newspaper instead. I learned that Punjab had sent thousands of soldiers to fight for the British Raj. They'd died defending Britain. Now the war had ended. The fighters that were alive had returned to discover their motherland more impoverished and less free than it was when they'd left. The Jallianwala Bagh massacre was their final reward!

Men gathered in our courtyard. The older ones who couldn't read asked Kanubhai to read the paper to them. They smoked bidis and talked. They forgot their work and ignored the April heat.

Women gathered in our front corridor.

"I wish our country would go back to its own peaceful way," Heeraben said. "Leave the Engrej alone and let them rule."

"Why should we?" I asked.

"Because they've been doing it for many years," she said.

"That's no excuse to let them continue. It's our country, and we are people, not lambs that can be led blindly to the slaughterhouse," Masi said. Her voice was full of passion and conviction. Like most Indians, the spilled blood of our countrymen had shaken Masi. She tucked her unruly hair behind her ears, wiped her eyes with the end of her sari, and said, "We are human beings just like the Engrej. They should never forget that."

As the discussion continued, it was clear that Heeraben didn't have many supporters.

I wrote in my diary, "Last year, when Jaya told me that our country was going through a transformation, I didn't think it was going to affect the people of Jamlee. It has, though. Our country could never go back to the old ways, because people want change, and demand it."

I tucked the diary back into the recessed window.

More news came pouring in the next day.

There was strict martial law in Punjab. Then, after an assault on a white woman in Amritsar, General Dyer issued a Crawling Order, which called for people to crawl on their hands and knees on the street where the woman had been assaulted. There were public floggings for disobeying the order.

Gandhiji urged the sarkar to let him visit Punjab, but he wasn't allowed there.

It was as if all of Jamlee felt Punjab's pain, humiliation, and sorrow. The massacre and what followed made us realize that the British did not value our lives. How could we support the Raj that had killed our own so mercilessly?

TWENTY-SIX

THE MORNING of my departure, I ate little, but my belly was as heavy as if I'd eaten a dozen mangoes along with their pits.

I asked Kaki if I could have my gold jewelry. She returned my things wrapped in the same handkerchief she had taken them away in.

I opened the knots and fingered my gold earrings, necklace, bangles, and silver toe rings. The metal was cold and shiny. I took out the bangles and handed the handkerchief and the rest of my things back to Kaki.

"You said I could give these to anyone I wanted. You probably meant Kanubhai or Jaya's children, though. With your permission, I'd like to give these to Shani's daughter," I said.

If Kaki was surprised by my request, she didn't show it. "They're yours to give."

I found Shani in the back courtyard shelling beans. As soon as she saw me, she got up, letting the beans fall from her hands. I hugged her, and tears ran down our faces.

"Hold my baby before you go," Shani said.

Lakha brought me the baby swaddled in a blanket. I held her for a while, kissed her forehead, then slipped the bangles on her hand, and handed her back to Shani.

"Leelabon!" was all Shani could say before she began to cry again.

"Take care of her," I said.

She nodded, wiping her tears with the back of her hand. Lakha did the same.

"I'll write you. Will you write back?" I asked Shani.

"Ho've," she said. "Send me homework, too." Then she put her arm around my waist. "The house will be empty without you."

"I'll be back soon. When you were gone, I missed you, too. I wanted to talk to you, ask questions, tell you the news."

She laughed. "Leelabon, you're saying this to make me feel better."

"Have you forgotten how rude I was when you first came? I'm the same Leela."

"You're not," she whispered.

Then I said good-bye to Dahi and the bullocks, to the kesuda and jamboo tree, to the roses and hibiscus flowers.

I visited each room of our house. I stood by the round window where I kept my notebook. I flipped through the pages filled with my thoughts.

I didn't take my notebook with me, but gave it to Kaki to put in my maju. Even if I didn't carry my words with me, I knew I would carry all the feelings behind them. It was enough.

I packed few clothes. Besides the silk chidri Saviben had given me, I took two light cotton ones, one heavy one, and a woolen vest, to keep me warm in the winter. Then I slipped the gold khilli in my pocket, hoping I'd never have to use it again.

That morning, Ba crumbled up several rotlis and mixed them with brown sugar and ghee. I helped her roll them into balls.

No one in town knew that I was leaving, not even Masi. "The fewer people know, the fewer tongues will wag," Kaki had said.

I was surprised that I wanted to see Masi one more time before I left. Something had happened during her last visit. I remembered how angry she had been after the Jallianwala Bagh massacre. How deeply she had felt for the victims. I hoped someday she might think differently about how widows should be treated. I was sorry I wasn't going to say good-bye to her. For now, it was better to go quietly.

Ba looked up the astrological chart and found an auspicious time for our departure. As Kanubhai and I got ready to leave, Ba was crying, not loudly, like she'd cried when Ramanlal had died, but softly, like a slightly misplaced roof tile dripping in monsoon.

With trembling hands, Ba filled the silver prayer lamp with ghee and a cotton wick and lighted it. I prayed to the elephant-headed Lord Ganesh to take obstacles out of my path, and then to Saraswati, the goddess of arts and knowledge.

Kaki and Kaka gave me a picture of the goddess Saraswati to take with me. Sitting on a peacock and clad in a white sari, she played the *veena*, a string instrument. I put the picture in my bag.

When I bowed to Kaka, he said, "Write me letters and tell me all about your new life."

I said, "Yes," thinking how quickly in the past year the gray army of old age and grief had taken over his dark hair completely.

Kaki said, "You make us proud. May you always be happy."

I thought it was a strange blessing to bestow upon

a widow, but it had come from her heart, and it could have magical power.

Ba held me tight.

Bapuji kept his hands behind his back and stood tall and straight, but I'd never seen so much pain on his face before.

I moved closer to him. "Don't worry about me. I'll study hard."

He rested both his hands on my shoulders; I could feel the weight of his hands and his gaze. The air between us stood mountain-still, and the words that Bapuji did not utter were written on it. I read them all.

As I turned around, the flame in the divi went out, and I took one deep, smoky breath before leaving.

Right outside the gate, Lakha had the bullock cart ready.

Before opening the gate, I glanced at my family again. My feet turned heavy.

Kanubhai put his right arm around my waist as if to say, *Time to go. No more looking back. Keep on moving.*

I sat in the cart. Once I left, the house would eat my family up with its silence, I thought. I glanced back once before Lakha said to the bullocks, "*Halo, mara vahala, halo,* walk, my dears, walk." And with their bells tinkling, the bullocks moved forward.

When we reached the station, Lakha took the luggage from the bullock cart and placed it on the train. He pressed his hands together and said to me, "*Vehla avajo,* come back soon."

"I will. Make sure Shani keeps reading."

He nodded and whispered, "May God protect you from all harms."

This was the first time I had traveled by train. The wheels were enormous and the carts that carried us were even bigger than I imagined. We walked all the way to the front and saw the engine, a coal-eating, fire-breathing, weight-pulling machine. Only after we got on the train did Lakha turn to go home. From the window of our compartment, I watched the bullocks and the cart as they slowly swayed back toward Jamlee.

"How long before we get there?" I asked Kanubhai.

"The train hasn't started yet, and you're asking me when we'll get there? Go to sleep and the time will go by quickly."

"I'm going to stay up and see everything."

There was a whistle, a slight jolt, and then the train started moving. I stared out the window, toward Jamlee, until the train picked up speed and a new horizon appeared outside. I watched as the farms and animals sped by me. Beyond that, forests thick with trees stood some distance from the track.

Before I knew it, my eyes had become heavy. I fell asleep, resting my head on Kanubhai's shoulder and woke up every time the shrill whistle blew. When we reached Ahmedabad, my hands were covered with fine soot and my eyes were stinging.

The station was bustling with people as if someone were getting married. I saw an Engrej as white as freshly picked cotton. How could such skin hold any sun? I saw several men in saffron robes with wooden bowls. I wondered if Fat Soma was among them. I scanned each face, but he wasn't there. I saw women in fancy saris like the ones Saviben used to wear. I didn't see any other widows. Were there no widows in the city? Or did they stay inside?

I reached out and grabbed Kanubhai's hand.

"Where are you taking me?" I asked.

"You have a few choices, and I want you to see the different schools and decide where you want to study."

"I want to go to the Sabarmati Ashram first."

"Then we'll go there." He looked into my eyes. "Are you ready to make your future?"

"I am," I replied evenly.

An event can alter a person or a nation. When Ramanlal passed away, my life changed and it forced me on an unusual journey. The massacre in Punjab stirred the nation against British rule. Gandhiji was traveling all over the country making speeches, bringing people together, and organizing satyagrah.

The people were listening and responding. Many successful lawyers, like Dr. Rajendra Prasad, had given up their lucrative practices to join Gandhiji. The Nobel Laureate Rabindranath Tagore had returned his knighthood to the King-Emperor in protest.

I wondered if traditions bound people as foreign rule had bound our country. Even when they hurt us, we could not leave them, because we were so used to them.

Two men and three women in white khadi clothes came from behind and walked past us. Their steps were firm and their strides were long, as if they wanted to accomplish so much. Were these the people making a different destiny for our country?

Was it time to join them?

I took a step.

GLOSSARY

AAREE: oh

AARTI: a group prayer involving the lighting of lamps and singing of hymns

AAVEE: coming. (I'm coming)

ABHLA: tiny mirrors sewn on fabric

ANGARKHA: a long, white, coatlike shirt

ANU: a ceremony performed for a bride before she goes to live with her husband

ARITHA: a tropical fruit. It foams like soapsuds when boiled in water

ASHRAM: a communal living place

BA: mother

BAJARI: pearl millet cultivated in India and Africa since prehistoric times

BAPUJI: father

BEELADEE: cat

BESS: sit

BHAGAVAD GITA: a religious classic of Hinduism. It is a part of Mahabharat.

BHAJANS: devotional songs

BHOOVA: a medicinal man who knows special chants to bring snake, scorpion, and other poisons out of a victim's body

BIDIS: cigarettes made from tobacco, wrapped in a leaf

BOR: a type of berry

BRAHMAN: a Hindu belonging to the highest caste

BUDDHU: dumb, one without intelligence

BURI: a dish made from the first milking of a buffalo after the birth of a calf

CHAL: let's go, come

CHALO: let's go, come (with respect)

CHANDLO: a dot made in the middle of the forehead of married women

CHAROLI: small, round nut

CHAUK: inner courtyard, usually paved with stones

CHEE, CHEE: very bad

CHIDRI: a widow's sari worn in Gujarat

CHOKDI: a village square, usually in the center of a small village or town

CHULA: clay stove

DAL: lentil soup

DALEEL: argument

DHARMA: duty

DHARMASHALA: a community hall, it also has guest rooms for visitors

DHOTI: a long piece of cloth wrapped around the waist and legs, resembles baggy trousers

DIVI: a brass or silver prayer lamp

DIWALI: the Hindu festival of lights

ENGREJ: an Englishman or English people

ENGREJI: English

FAJETO: soup made with mango pits, checkpea flour, and spices

GAYATRI MANTRA: one of the most scared mantras for Hindus

GHAGRI-POULKA: a long skirt and blouse

GHEE: clarified butter with a nutty flavor

HARTAL: strike

HASADI: a wide choker. It literally means "clavicle."

HOLI: the festival marking the beginning of spring

HO'VE: yes, sure (colloquial)

INDHONI: a ring of soft, padded material, used to carry water pots on the head

JALEBIS: sweets made of white flour, deep fried and soaked in sugar syrup

JAMBOO TREE: a large deciduous tree bearing plumlike fruits in monsoon

JANOI: a sacred thread worn by brahman men and boys, also the coming-of-age ceremony in which the thread is given

KADU TEA: a bitter herbal tea

KAKA: uncle who is the father's brother

KAKI: kaka's wife

KALOTAR: a deadly black snake

KANSAR: a steaming, whole-wheat and brown-sugar sweet drenched in ghee

KESUDA: a tropical tree, also known as "flame of the forest"

KHADI: rough, hand-spun cotton. Mahatma Gandhi wore hand-spun khadis.

KHARKHARO: mourning and visitation after death. In old times it lasted for days.

KHATLIS: bed frames made of teakwood and laced with sturdy jute strings

KHILLI: a nail or a metal pin with one sharp end

KICHUS: thin wafers made of cooked rice flour with cumin seeds and salt

KOTHIMDA: a fruit-bearing vine that grows in monsoon

LAKKH: shellac

LOO: a hot, dry summer wind

MADARI: a person who performs tricks with his pet snakes, a bear, or monkey

MAHABHARAT: the longest poem in world literature

MAJU: heavy wooden chest fitted with brass locks

MANBHATT: a copper pot player

MANJIRA: brass finger cymbals

MARJIVA: pearl divers

MASI: mother's sister

MENDHI: a tropical shrub whose leaves are used as a skin and hair dye

MOKSHA: nirvana

NESDO: a rabari camp

ODHANI: a scarf, usually two and a half yards long

PALAV: the end of a sari, usually ornate

PAPDI: fried, crisp chickpea wafers

PATLA: very low wooden stools to sit cross-legged on

PATRAL AND PADIO: a plate and bowl made out of the leaves of a *khakhra* tree

PENDA: a sweet candy made by boiling milk until it solidifies

PIPUL TREE: a fig tree indigenous to India

POORANPOLI: bread filled with sweetened lentils and cardamom

PRABHATI: devotional songs that people sing in the morning while doing chores

PUJA: a ceremonial worship

PUNDIT: a learned man, scholar

PYE: the smallest unit of currency at that time, like a penny

RAAND: means "widow," but used as a derogatory term

RABARI: once a nomadic tribe. Now they live in mud huts with thatched roofs.

RAJAI: very soft blanket

RAMJI MANDIR: Lord Rama Temple

RANGOLI: a floral or geometric design made to adorn the home during Diwali

RISHI: sage

ROTLI: a whole-wheat bread cooked on a stove

RUDRAKSH: a tropical tree considered holy. Beads are made out of its dried fruit.

SADHUS: holy men

SAGDI: small coal-burning stove

SAPTARSHI: the constellation of seven stars, the Big Dipper

SARKAR: government

SATCHITANAND: (sanskrit) made of three words: sat, chit, anand—meaning truth, conciousness, bliss

SATYAGRAH: the philosophy of peaceful resistance practiced by Mahatma Gandhi

SHAHEED: martyr

SHIMLA TREE: a tropical tree bearing seed pods filled with soft fibers

SHINGODA: a type of water chestnut

SHIROMANI: best of the best. Literally, the "jewel of the head"

SUKHADI: bars made out of whole-wheat flour, ghee, and brown sugar

TANPURA: a one-stringed instrument

THEPLA: whole-wheat bread spiced with cumin seeds and turmeric

TULSI: holy basil plant sacred to Hindus

VAKEEL: lawyer

VEENA: stringed musical instrument played by the goddess Saraswati

WIDHWA: a widow

YAMRAJ: god of death

When I was ten years old, I spent a few days with my great-aunt Maniba. She was a child widow, and just like Leela, she wore a chidri and had her head shaved. I kept thinking that she wasn't much older than me when she was widowed.

Maniba was born in 1888, so her life unfolded earlier than Leela's, but her struggles were the same. It was a time when girls in Gujarat didn't attend school beyond fourth or fifth grade, and widows were shunned and ignored by society for the rest of their lives. After becoming a widow, Maniba pleaded, fought, and finally convinced her parents (my great-grandparents) to let her go to Ahmedabad to continue her studies. What tremendous courage it must have taken! After finishing college, she returned to her home town of Kapadvanj and became the principal of the Kanya Shala, girls' school.

From childhood, I have admired Narmad, the great poet, essayist, and social reformer who preceded Mahatma Gandhi by several decades. His ideas and ideals for equality of sexes, abolition of the caste system, and national pride were much ahead of their time. Gandhiji was a Gujarati, and from early on his influence was strong in Gujarat. I grew up reading Gandhian literature, and most of my teachers were freedom fighters who participated in satyagrah. Naturally, I wanted Narmad and Gandhiji to shape Leela's thoughts, and for her journey to parallel that of India's struggle for independence.

In the last four years of my father's life, he told me details of the society and community of early Gandhi-era Gujarat. His mother had passed away when he was nine, and his grandmother and widowed aunt, Maniba, raised him, so he was able to pass their stories on to me. Leela's story is a tribute to Maniba and countless other child widows who suffered needlessly.

Many thanks to the following people for their help:

The team at Hyperion and all my family, friends, and colleagues.

And especially Georgia Beaverson, Donna Bray, Judy Bryan, Jalaj Dani,
Vita Dani, Arianne Lewin, Roseanne Lindsay, Julie Shaull,
Charlotte Sheedy, Neha Sheth, Rajan Sheth, Melinda Starkweather, Amit
Trivedi, Bharatiben Trivedi, Rohit Trivedi, Susan Trivedi, Joey Valdez,
Rupa Valdez, Jacqueline Woodson, and Bridget Zinn.

DISCUSSION GUIDE

Disney • HYPERION BOOKS

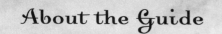

About the Guide

This guide includes discussion questions intended to provoke thought and insight into the themes of the book which include hope, sacrifice, nonviolence, family obligation, education, and social change.

Discussion Questions

1   When the novel opens, Leela is most concerned about what things in her life? What is important to her? What are her plans for the future? Who made these plans?

2   Describe the family living arrangements in Leela's home. What would be great about living with an extended family? What would be difficult? Which member is Leela closest to? Why? Who would you most like to live with in your extended family?

3   Who is Ramanlal? What kind of relationship does Leela have with him as the novel opens? What glimpse does the reader get of her future life as his bride? Do you think they would have been happy together? How is that future destroyed?

4   What are the customs surrounding death in Leela's Brahman community? Which ones are particularly difficult for her to surrender to? Which ones would be most difficult for you?

5   What exactly is "keeping corner"? Why must Leela uphold the traditions of her family and community? What consequences will she and her family face if she does not? Does her brother agree with these customs, or not? Why?

6   What is Leela's only opportunity for a future other than keeping corner? Who takes her on a journey though she is not permitted to leave her house? At first Leela is not very interested in studying. How does this change over the course of the novel? How does Saviben make the year bearable for Leela?

7   Leela begins following the new ideas of Gandhiji (known as Gandhi in the Western world) as he leads his people into a series of protests through nonviolence. How do Gandhi and other writers make Leela begin to question her destiny?

8   At what price did Leela's family keep the *satyagraha*? Did Leela believe it was worth the sacrifice? How could there be "a victory in the defeat"? How does Leela's family compare in wealth and circumstance to most of their countrymen?

9   Why is Leela suddenly jealous of Lakha's new wife, Shani? How does Leela treat her at first? Does the growth and blossoming of their friendship show what changes in Leela? What does Leela learn from Shani that makes her suffering particularly hard to bear? Shani brings out the best in Leela; which friends do that for you?

10 Discuss Leela's relationship with her brother, Kanubhai. How does he work on her behalf? What sacrifices does he make for her? Why do her parents feel powerless to act on her behalf?

Projects

Language Arts

As you read the novel, write at least five journal entries as if you are Leela. Avoid summarizing events; make it sound as if she is writing the journal herself.

Character Chart

Fill in the graphic organizer about the many changes you see in Leela over the course of the novel.

	Physical	Social	Intellectual
Beginning			
Ending			

History

Study the *satyagraha* movement that was led by Gandhi. Create a timeline about what you learned and illustrate it with your own pictures or those from other sources.

Research the caste system in India. In a journal response, describe not just what you learned, but also your response to the limitations it places on individuals.

Author Interview

1 Your great-aunt, Maniben Trivedi, inspired this novel. How did you come to know and share her story?

I remembered meeting my father's aunt Maniben when I was nine years old at our ancestral home in a small town in Gujarat. Dressed in *chidri* with a shaved head, she had a commanding voice and left a lasting impression on me. I realized that she was not much older than I was when she had become a widow.

When I started writing a few years ago my parents encouraged me to tell her story. Since my father's mother died when he was young, Maniben raised him, and he told me how, after she became a widow, she argued and convinced her parents to send her to school in Ahmedabad. Eventually, she returned to her hometown and became the principal of a girls' school. My mother also grew up with a great-aunt who was a widow, and knew much about a widow's life and suffering in that time.

I was also fortunate to visit my ancestral home in 2003. As I walked the streets, they brought the stories my parents had told me alive. I could picture young Leela wandering those dusty streets and sitting in a corner of the house for a year.

Our family has always told stories. This tradition of sharing our ancestors' journeys has been a driving force behind my writing, and I am fortunate to share it with the readers.

2   What's your favorite part of the writing process? What would you avoid if you could?

My favorite part of the writing process is to first get the story on the page without stopping. In this story it was difficult to do so because the historical facts and events had to be interwoven in the story. It took me a lot longer to write this book than my first two novels, but it has been a very fulfilling project.

When you try to get the story out as quickly as you can, it is hard to avoid mistakes. If I could, I would get the plot, voice, and scenes right the first time so I wouldn't have to go back and add things, but it is impossible for me to do so.

3   What are you working on now?

I am working on a couple of young adult novels. I'm done with the research for one of them and have started writing it. I also have a second picture book coming out next year.

This guide was created by Tracie Vaughn Zimmer, a reading specialist and children's author. Visit her Web site at www.tracievaughnzimmer.com to find hundreds of other guides to children's and young adult literature.

——— Also by Kashmira Sheth ———

Keeping Corner

ISBN-978-0-7868-3859-2
$15.99

**Koyal Dark,
Mango Sweet**

ISBN-978-0-7868-3857-8
$15.99

ISBN-978-0-7868-3858-5
$7.99

Blue Jasmine

ISBN-978-0-7868-1855-6
$15.99

ISBN-978-0-7868-5565-0
$5.99

DISNEY • HYPERION BOOKS
An imprint of Disney Book Group
114 Fifth Avenue, New York, NY 10011
Visit us at www.hyperionteens.com